Small bug in the snow

TOM GATES
EXTRA
SPECIAL TREATS
(not)

By Liz Pichon
(who likes treats)

Treat

Not a treat

Scholastic Canada Ltd.

Scholastic Canada Ltd.
604 King Street West, Toronto, Ontario M5V 1E1, Canada

Scholastic Inc.
557 Broadway, New York, NY 10012, USA

Scholastic Australia Pty Limited
PO Box 579, Gosford, NSW 2250, Australia

Scholastic New Zealand Limited
Private Bag 94407, Botany, Manukau 2163, New Zealand

Scholastic Children's Books
Euston House, 24 Eversholt Street, London NW1 1DB, UK

www.scholastic.ca

Library and Archives Canada Cataloguing in Publication

Pichon, Liz, author
Extra special treats (not) / by Liz Pichon (who likes treats).

(Tom Gates)
ISBN 978-1-4431-3934-2 (pbk.)

I. Title. II. Series: Pichon, Liz. Tom Gates.

PZ7.P53Ext 2015   j823'.92   C2014-904510-7

Copyright © 2013 by Liz Pichon.
First published in the UK by Scholastic Children's Books, 2013.
This edition published by Scholastic Canada Ltd., 2015.

All rights reserved.
No part of this publication
may be reproduced or
stored in a retrieval system,
or transmitted in any form or
by any means, electronic, mechanical,
recording, or otherwise, without
written permission of the publisher,
Scholastic Canada Ltd.,
604 King Street West,
Toronto, Ontario
M5V 1E1, Canada.
In the case of photocopying or
other reprographic copying,
a licence must be obtained
from Access Copyright
(Canadian Copyright
Licensing Agency),
1 Yonge Street, Suite 800,
Toronto, Ontario M5E 1E5
(1-800-893-5777).

6 5 4 3 2 1   Printed in Canada   139   15 16 17 18 19

THIS is a STAR PUPIL BADGE.

It's not mine, it belongs to MARCUS MELDREW. I found it under my desk and picked it up.

He hasn't noticed it's gone yet.

The (BADGE) must have fallen off

O his jumper.

I am going to give it back to him (eventually).

Mr Fullerman made Marcus a **STAR PUPIL**

because he'd done all his homework on time and

apparently he's been **making a BIG effort in class.**

Marcus hasn't stopped BRAGGING about

his (BADGE) ever since he put it on.

Look at my badge.

AMY's had a **STAR PUPIL BADGE** before but

I haven't (YET).

Mr Fullerman chooses different **STAR PUPILS**

every term. I've noticed that if you have a

STAR PUPIL BADGE TEACHERS are NICER and smile

a lot more at you. It's TRUE! ☺

Teachers smiling

AND you get to hang out in the library at lunchtimes (which would be excellent for catching up on my comic reading).

The badges this term l👀k EXCELLENT.

So, just for a change, I'm going to get ALL my 📖 homework done on time too. 🙂

I REALLY want a (BADGE).

In the meantime, here's a picture of Marcus when he thought he'd LOST his badge. And here's a picture of Marcus when he got the badge back.

AGH!

Grumpy face →

Marcus didn't even say thank you to me. **S**o I did this doodle of him for FUN.

Tom, if you put as much EFFORT into your homework as you have into your doodles, you'll be well on the way to becoming a STAR PUPIL.

Mr Fullerman

Yes, Mr Fullerman, I WILL. :)

(I've said it now.)

I'm walking home from school with Derek (my **BEST** friend and next-door neighbour). We're chatting about all kinds of important STUFF like:

★ What we're going to EAT when we get home and toast

★ who's going to get a **STAR PUPIL** **BADGE** this time.

Then we **spot** someone in front of us who looks a bit like my grumpy older sister, Delia.

Is that Delia? Derek asks me.

And I say, I'm not sure, it might be?

"DEEEEELLLLLIA!... DEEEEELLLLLIA!..."

I shout - but she IGNORES me.

"She can't hear me," I say.

"Let's shout LOUDER," Derek suggests.

"And get a bit closer too," I say.

So we do...

From the lOOk on Delia's face, I think she heard us that time.
I <u>was</u> going to say hello - but I changed my mind ... quickly.   Uh oh

I'm not sure Delia was
THAT pleased to see us.

Grrrrrr

We run ≡ all the way home instead.
"Your sister wasn't very happy, was she?"
Derek says as he goes into his house.
"Don't worry," I tell him.
"Delia's NEVER happy, she ALWAYS looks like that."   (Which is true.)

Delia in the morning.   Delia in the afternoon.   Delia in the evening.

Then we both say, (BYE) and (See you later.)

And I go inside.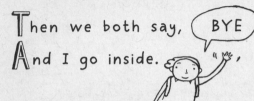

As soon as I close the door,

I forget all about Delia and head

straight for the kitchen, because I've just

remembered that Mum bought a GIANT

packet of Chocolate Raisins the other day.

(Mmm mmm mmm.)

The trouble is, Mum often hides the really good **TREATS**.

This is because:

1. **T**REATS get eaten STRAIGHT AWAY in our house.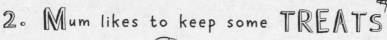

2. **M**um likes to keep some **TREATS** JUST for guests  (Biscuits?) (which is annoying).

3. I'm **NOT** supposed to help myself. **LUCKILY** I've become an EXPERT at finding them.

(Mmmmmm, let me see.) That didn't take long.

RESULT

The trick is to OPEN the raisins carefully without RIPPING the packet so it doesn't look like anyone's touched them.
(Gently does it.)

I'm SO busy delicately tipping the raisins into my hand that I don't HEAR Mum coming downstairs - until she's outside the kitchen door.

THEN I PANIC.

There's just enough time to SHOVE the packet of raisins back inside the teapot and SLAM down the lid before Mum comes in.

"HELLO, TOM, you're home early," Mum says.

(I'm trying not to look guilty.)

I tell Mum, "Derek and I ran ALL the way home *EXTRA FAST* in a race. PHEW! I feel REALLY TIRED now."

(The bit about being "TIRED" I've added in for a VERY good reason.)

I'm still holding the chocolate raisins in my hand and they're beginning to MELT

I do a MASSIVE YAWN

and put my hand UP to my mouth.

Then I SHOVE IN as many of the raisins as I can without Mum noticing.

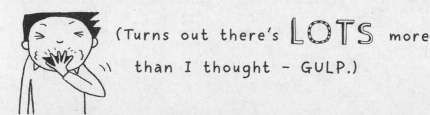

(Turns out there's LOTS more than I thought - GULP.)

This plan would have worked, but Mum keeps asking me questions. She says,

"You know Granny Mavis and Granddad Bob are coming round tonight to keep an eye on things?"

I can't speak because my mouth is STUFFED full of chocolate raisins.

So I NOD my head instead.

"We're going out for dinner with someone Dad works with." I smile and nod some more.

"I've got this new dress especially for tonight - oh - AND Granny Mavis doesn't need to cook; there's food in the oven." (Which is a relief because you never know what Granny will make.)

Pasta and peaches, anyone?

I'm trying REALLY hard to chew the raisins without Mum noticing. SLOWLY SLOWLY

Are you eating something, Tom?

(That didn't work, then.)

When I try and say NOTHING a raisin nearly POPS out of my mouth.

Instead, I do the ONLY thing I can think of to get me out of this

VERY
TRICKY
SITUATION.

Here goes...

I give Mum a GREAT BIG HUG.

"That's a nice hug, Tom ... what's that for?"
Mum says, hugging me back.
All the time I'm chewing raisins and TRYING
to think of a good answer.

16

Then **SUDDENLY** Delia comes STORMING INTO the house and 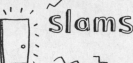 **slams** the front door behind her.

"Where's Tom?"

She sounds a bit cross.

 "What's wrong, Delia?"

Mum asks her.

"**THIS** is what's **WRONG!**"

Delia holds up her **BROKEN** mobile phone.

"IT'S all **YOUR FAULT!**"

she says, pointing at me.

(17)

"**W**hat have I done?" I say, trying to finish off the last raisin.

(I keep close to Mum in case Delia goes even more "**BONKeRS**".)

Mum says, "How could Tom break your phone? He's been here with me."

Good point, Mum.

Delia is STILL looking **FiERCE**

"**I**'ll tell you **how** - Tom and that nerdy friend of his *sneaked* right up behind me and **SCREAMED** MY NAME so loudly the **SHOCK** made me drop my PHONE. **NOW** look at it!"

(Who knew that would happen?)

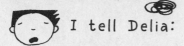 I tell Delia:

1. **D**erek isn't NERDY. (Derek NOT being NERDY.)

2. **B**reaking her phone was an accident.

Then I do an EXTRA sad face to make the point a bit more.

"We only wanted to say hello!" I tell Mum.

Delia is SCOWLING at me.

She says,

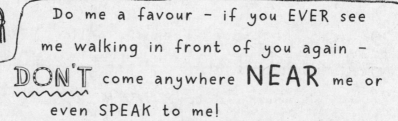

Do me a favour — if you EVER see me walking in front of you again — DON'T come anywhere NEAR me or even SPEAK to me!

"**C**alm down, Delia," Mum says, which winds her up even more.

"I'm sure **T**om didn't **mean** to break your phone. Did you, Tom?"

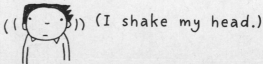 (I shake my head.)

"We could get it fixed?" Mum adds.

Delia **SLAMS** her phone down on the table and says, "Good luck with that," then *STORMS* off in a huff.

LOOking at the cracked phone on the table, I tell Mum,

"It's definitely BROKen now."

"Oh dear," Mum says. Then she notices the time. "Tom, would you please go and tell your dad to *hurry up*. We mustn't be late tonight. I bet he's still working in his shed!"

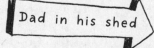

Dad in his shed

zzzzzzz

(He's not.)

"Yes, Mum," I say while trying NOT TO STARE at the 👀--- teapot.

"I don't want Delia being in such a **BAD** MOOD when Bob and Mavis get here. She can use my phone until we get her a NEW one. Or get hers fixed."

(Well, that's not going to happen, is it?)

If you ask ME, it seems a bit unfair that Delia gets a new PHONE. If I break something, that NEVER happens to ME.

NOW might be a good time to ask about my BROKEN bike?

Mum, my watch is broken

Never mind

If Delia's getting a new phone, can I have a NEW bike?

Mmmmmmm

(That'll be a NO then.) Sigh.

Delia is an EXPERT at blaming ME
for things she's done. She did it ALL the time
when I was little.

Her favourite trick was pinching my food
when I wasn't l👀king. ESPECIALLY ice cream.

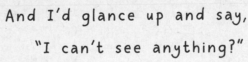

Delia would stare at something
in the air and say,

"What's that, Tom?"

And I'd glance up and say,

"I can't see anything?"

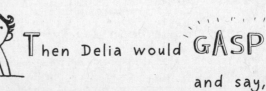 Then Delia would GASP

and say,

"Look up THERE!
Can't you see it ... it's a **BUG** or
something!"

I loved BUGS, so
that would make me
STARE even more.

"Over there, QUICKLY, LOOK!

LOOK!"

While I was busy looking at NOTHING, Delia
would be sneakily *LEANING* over and taking
GIANT LICKS of my ice cream. Then she'd
say, "Didn't you see it? Never mind — it's gone
now, Tom."

(Along with half my

ice cream usually.)

Ha!
Ha!

I was only young, so it took me a while to work out what she was doing.

And if I tried the same trick on Delia she'd just say, "Don't bother, Tom, I'm not an idiot ... like you."

She always was a nice sister.

Look up there ↑

(Not.)

While Mum is giving her phone to Delia, I'm sitting here STILL STARING at the teapot filled with *Chocolate Raisins.*

I should be sensible and stay away from the raisins. ESPECIALLY after such a

LUCKY ESCAPE.

BUT THEY ARE DELICIOUS!

So I'm thinking...

☺ Will Mum be gone for very long? (YES) ✓

☺ Have I got time to GRAB another handful of raisins? (YES) ✓

As the answer to BOTH questions is (YES!) I lift the teapot lid and scoop out another handful of *Chocolate* Raisins.

Then another...

Then one more for luck!

I don't hear Dad coming in from the shed until he says,

"A HA!" which makes me **JUMP!** "THAT'S where the raisins are. I've been looking for them everywhere. You haven't eaten them all, have you, **Tom?"** Dad takes the packet from me to see for himself. (Surprisingly, I've eaten quite a few.)

"I'm guessing your mum didn't say you could help yourself, did she?" (I've been rumbled.)

I tell Dad, "It was a small packet, I haven't eaten *THAT* many."

(I think I'm in trouble.)

Then Dad says,

It was a tiny packet of raisins

26

"I can buy another packet to replace this one."
And he tips the rest of the raisins

RIGHT into his mouth.

"MMMMM, I love raisins," he says while tilting his head back to finish them off. Mum comes in just in time to see the last one being eaten.

And you wonder WHY I HIDE the treats in this house?

Dad can't answer because his mouth is stuffed full of raisins. GULP

"You know we're going out for dinner?"

"I'm still hungry, don't worry!" Dad tells her.

"The WHOLE PACKET'S gone?" Mum says.

 (Dad doesn't mention that I helped him out.)

EXTRA
SPECIAL BOARD GAMES

THE FOSSILS arrive just in time to take Mum's mind off the missing treats. Their MOBILITY SCOOTER has packed up so it takes them a lot longer than usual to get to our house.

"We made a few changes in case it snows. Which didn't really work," Granny Mavis tells Mum.

Can't see →

"Well, I'm glad you're here and in one piece," Mum tells them both.

Granddad has brought some **BOARD GAMES** for us to play, while Granny Mavis has some

serious knitting to do.

"**A**re you up for a **BOARD GAME CHALLENGE, Tom?**" Granddad asks me.

"As long as you don't **CHEAT**, Granddad."

"**ME CHEAT - NEVER!**"

he says, pretending to be **SHOCKED**.

(He does cheat, but in a funny way.)

Granny Mavis says,

"I've heard the weather's going to get really COLD, so I'm knitting with EXTRA-thick wool this year - SEE!"

Clickity clack
clickity clack

Granny's **KNITTING** is a bit like her `cooking` - unusual. Some of her jumpers are quite handy if you need **EXTRA** pockets.

Others don't work out so well.

I'm NOT sure it works, Granny.

Mum shows **THE FOSSILS** where everything is (as if they don't know already).

- There's the cooker

She mentions that **Delia's** a bit fed up
because her phone's **BROKEN**.

"You might not see much of her tonight,"
Mum says.

Which is **GOOD** NEWS, if you ask me.

Granddad wonders if a game of **S**nakes and **L**adders would cheer Delia up?

"I don't think so, Granddad," I say.

I'm not five, get lost

"Just you and me,
then," Granddad says.

"**YESSS!**" I say while
getting out the board.

Mum carries on chatting.

"We won't be late tonight. Besides, as you can
see, Frank has eaten already."

Mum is STARING at the
empty packet of raisins.

Empty

Dad expertly changes the subject by saying,

"Is that a new dress, Rita?

It looks LOVELY."

Which makes Mum laugh.

Then Granny tells her,

"That pale colour

really suits you."

Mum smiles.

"Do you think so? I'd better NOT

spill anything on it tonight.

 A BIG STAIN

on this dress

would be a

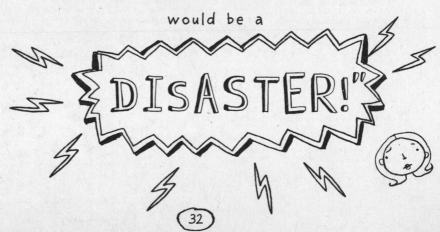 DISASTER!"

Ha!
Ha!

Dad is holding Mum's coat for her and wants
to get going.

"We'll be off now. Be good, Tom."

"I'm always GOOD!"
I remind them and wave.

Mum and Dad both say BYE and head
out of the door.
And that's when I SPOT something on
the BACK of Mum's nice
NEW PALE-COLOURED DRESS
that I'm guessing wasn't
there when she bought it.

— Uh oh

MY HANDPRINT
in chocolate

I must have left it when I hugged her. If Mum
sees that stain, it really would
be a **DISASTER**, for me!
I'll just have to make sure I'm in
bed before they get home. (It's a good plan.)

Gulp—

Delia is still sulking in her room. So it's nice

and PEACEFUL for Granddad and me to play

Snakes and Ladders and some of the other

games he's brought.

"Shall we **WARM** up with a memory

game first?" he suggests. This is one of

Granddad's favourites. He's got a very good

memory for someone who's a bit OLD.

Here's how you play the game:

Use a tray to put some objects on.

You have FIVE MINUTES

to look at them –

then you cover the tray *over* with something.

(Like a tea towel.) I've learnt not to leave

Granddad on his own for too

long. He likes SWAPPING

things around on the tray. OR if he's being really

sneaky he'll add more stuff when I'm not looking.

After covering the tray, you take turns trying
to remember as many objects as you can.
So far we've got:

Smelly sock

An apple

A pencil

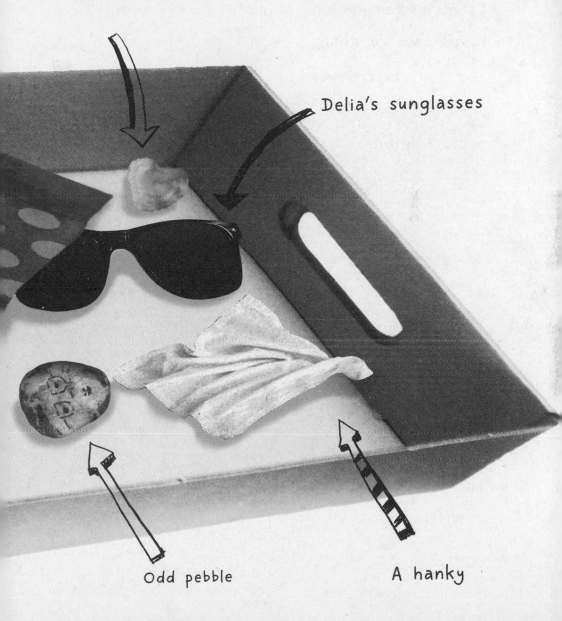

"What's THAT?" I ask him.

"It's a pebble I found that I think looks like your granny."

(It does look a bit like her.)

It's a good selection of stuff.

Let's PLAY, Granddad says.

I just NOD because if I talk I might FORGET something. We're both STARING at the TRAY and I'm trying to get all the things into → my HEAD.

Then Granddad says, Guess what I've brought us for a treat?

That's the other thing Granddad does. He asks me questions, which makes me forget stuff.
I shrug my shoulders and keep concentrating.

 "Caramel wafers for **BOTH** of us," he says.

 "**YES!**"

I'm **SO** excited about the 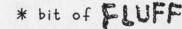 wafers I've already forgotten **HALF** of what's on the tray.

I'll have a go anyway.

"On the tray there is ...

* bit of **FLUFF**
* a sock
* a hanky ...
* errrrrrrmmmmm, a pencil?"

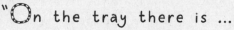

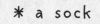

I do my best but I'm sure I've missed a few out. Then it's Granddad's turn. I think he's remembered a **LOT** more things than I did.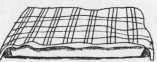
He's talking in a silly voice so it's hard to tell. "Last buwt nowt weast ... caramwel wafers ... and teef."

TEETH? "I don't remember there being any 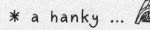 TEETH on the tray?" I tell Granddad.

He takes the tea towel OFF the
tray and sure enough there
are ... some

TEETH. →

"Towld you there were
TEEF," he says, popping his
teeth back in. Very funny, Granddad.
He says we should eat our wafers, so we
both start unwrapping them.
Then Granny Mavis says from the kitchen,

Don't eat those wafers NOW; you'll spoil
your dinner.

Groa

This is the perfect time to show Granddad
how to do the caramel-wafer biscuit trick*.
That way it won't look like we've
eaten them.

Empty wafer

*See page 43, The Brilliant World of Tom Gates, for how to do the WAFER BISCUIT TRICK.

I'm SO busy eating my wafer that I nearly forget to tell Granny she doesn't need to cook. In between mouthfuls I shout out,  "Mum's made dinner already, Granny – it's in the oven."

JUST in time too because she calls back,

Oh, that's a shame! I was going to make you my Chicken and Cornflakes Surprise!

Granny sounds a tiny bit disappointed.

(I'm not. I don't fancy chicken and cornflakes right now ... or ever.)

Something starts to smell tasty, which is good news.

The smell of food cooking finally brings Delia downstairs

(she's still grumpy, though).

She's using Mum's phone → to call all her friends and tell them:

"My annoying little brother blah blah ..

SCREAMED at me so LOUDLY I dropped my phone. It's TOTALLY smashed to pieces now."

I have to listen to her **EXAGGERATING** everything that happened.

Which is VERY annoying. ☹

I try and ignore her by having a *SPEEDY* game of Snakes and Ladders with Granddad. (He won.)

While we wait for dinner, I do a quick bit of drawing too. Dinner smells yummy. All my doodles have FOOD in them, which is making my tummy rumble even more.

Granny Mavis calls out, Dinner's NEARLY READY.

It seems to be taking **AGES?**

I show Granddad how to draw a MONSTER

like this one.

He's drawn his own

monster, which is **FUNNY.**

GRANNYSAURUS

"It's a GRANNYSAURUS,"

he tells me, just as

Granny calls out, FOOD UP!

Which makes me 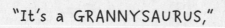**RUSH** into the kitchen ...

... to see **THIS**. Which is a surprise!
↓

No wonder DINNER took so **long**.

I think it's chicken and rice? It's hard to tell.

Delia is still chatting on her "new" phone.

She says, "I have **NO** idea what it is;

I'll send you a photo so you can

guess."

Granny Mavis is very cheerful and says,

"ENJOY!" (I'll have a go.)

EXTRA SPECIAL STORIES

When Mum and Dad AREN'T here, I like to ask THE FOSSILS QUESTIONS about stuff that NORMALLY I wouldn't be allowed to. Questions like:

- 🙂 Was Dad a REALLY naughty little kid?
- 🙂 Did he do all his homework?
- 🙂 Was he rubbish at ~~Spelin~~ spelling?
- 🙂 Who's your favourite son – Dad or Uncle Kevin?

(They never answer that one.)

Today I want to know, "What was Dad like as a baby?" Granny Mavis thinks for a while and says,

Well, let me see.

 "Your dad was a

VERY HAIRY baby."

I wasn't expecting **THAT** answer.

"Was he? How **HAIRY**?"

 "He had a big mop of hair on his **head**,"
Granny Mavis remembers.

"That's gone now," Delia mutters.

 "And he had **HAIR** on his back too."

"That's just WEIRD,"  says Delia.

I want to know MORE.

"Did he look like a baby

 **WEREWOLF?"** ⟹ Grrrrrrrrrrrr

Granny laughs. ha! ha!

"No - his hair was lovely and Soft and FLUFFY."

"That's not a baby, that's a KITTEN."

Delia is shaking her head.

"Frank didn't stay hairy for very long," Granny Mavis adds.

"My family are all FREAKS,"

Delia is muttering.

"I'm not a freak," I tell her.

"That's a matter of opinion," Delia says.

I ignore Delia and ask Granny Mavis something else.

"Was Uncle Kevin a HAIRY baby too?"

"Not like your dad. Kevin was quite a cute baby."

"NOW that is a surprise," Delia murmurs.

I make the most of THE FOSSILS being very chatty tonight and ask a few more things while I can.

"**I**s it true that Uncle **K**evin ALWAYS got Dad into trouble?"

(Just like Delia does with me.) ☹

"**S**ometimes that happened,"
Granddad tells me and laughs.

"**D**ad said it happened ALL the time,"
I tell Granddad.

"I remember they used to have rolling-downhill races in the park. Kevin ALWAYS wanted to **WIN.**"
* ☆ *

"Nothing's changed there,"
Delia whispers to me.
Granddad carries on.
"**F**rank kept coming FIRST

so Kevin decided that this time he'd give him a
SHOVE in the wrong direction...

He made Frank roll right into ALL the long GRASS ...

Frank

... which was **FULL** OF stinging nettles and thistles. Not great when you're only wearing shorts like Frank was."

"Sounds itchy,"
I say to Granddad.

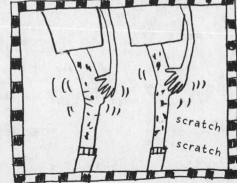

scratch

scratch

"It was."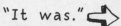

Then Granny Mavis tells us how LOVELY it is that both brothers get on so well NOW. Which is only SORT of true. So I say, "They kind of get on."

Delia prods me with her foot. "What do you mean, Tom?" Granny asks. "Uncle Kevin drives Dad NUTS," I explain. "Especially when he does things like this." I do an impression of Uncle Kevin talking to Dad.

"'Hello, Frank, what's under the hat - oh lOOk, nothing!' Dad doesn't like that AT ALL."

I don't mention ALL the other things Dad gets cross about to THE FOSSILS (there's too many). Delia is mouthing the word FOOL at me. Which is irritating, but it reminds me to mention the two caramel wafers I saved especially for her.

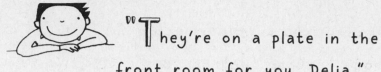 "They're on a plate in the front room for you, Delia."

She's suspicious but takes them anyway.

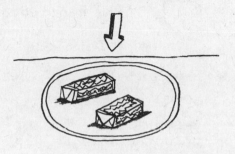

Watching Delia falling for the Empty Wafer Biscuit Trick always makes me laugh.

He! He! Ha! Ha!

Hilarious, Tom___

Granddad and I have one more game of Snakes and Ladders Ooow

(I win this time).

Then I head off to bed EARLY

because I don't want to be around when

Mum and Dad get back.

On the way to bed Granny tells me it's their

FIFTIETH *

*

wedding anniversary soon.

"We should ALL do something

together to CELEBRATE."

"LET'S GO TO A THEME PARK!"

I suggest helpfully.

"I'm not sure Granddad could go on a rollercoaster!

I promise, we'll do something nice,"

Granny tells me as she turns

out the lights.

Granddad's
teeth

(Good point,
Granny)

As I'm **not** that sleepy at all,
I wait until Granny Mavis is downstairs,
then go to my bedroom window to show Derek
the DOODLE I did earlier. ➡

(He thinks it's funny.)
When I SPOT 👀

Mum and Dad's car 🚗 pulling

up outside, I'm forced to JUMP ➤

back into bed *QUICKLY*.

I can hear them chatting downstairs while
I'm pretending to be asleep.

zzzzzzzz

Mum has said the word (DISASTER)

quite a few times. Which is a worry.

I close my eyes even ↘ ↙ TIGHTER just in

case anyone comes into my room. With any luck

Mum will have forgotten all about the

🖐 HANDprint stain on her dress by

the morning.

I REALLY HOPE SO. ☺

53

THIS is the **FIRST** thing I see when I come downstairs in the morning.

There might as well be a **MASSIVE** SIGN that says:

LOOK WHAT **TOM** did. **HE'S** iN BIG TRouBLE!

(I hope not.)

I'll go to Derek's house EARLY and walk to school with him, to avoid any awkward questions.

As I'm getting ready, Dad comes back from his morning run and says, "Hi, Tom. You're up early — everything OK?"

And I say, "Is it early? I hadn't noticed."

I don't want to look DESPERATE to leave, so I ask Dad if they had a nice time last night.

"We had a great time, and I didn't have to pay for dinner, which is always good news."

(Here comes the **BAD** news ... gulp.)

"But the **BAD** news is ..." (Groan.)

"... your mother's new dress got a STAIN on it."

Exhibit one

(AND IT'S ALL YOUR FAULT, TOM.)

Then Dad carries on...

"There was something on the chair she sat on at the restaurant - so they've offered to clean the dress!"

I say, "YES!"

STAIN

Which takes Dad by surprise.

I tell Dad, "I'm happy for Mum" as an explanation in case he gets suspicious.

Then Dad's phone rings. I can tell he's talking to Uncle Kevin because of the **faces** he pulls. He's tapping his watch and shaking his head. Which means "why's he calling SO early?" Dad's rolling his eyes now.

"Yes ... yes ... yes..." he says.

"We'd love to see you all later, then, Kevin."

Then he hangs up.

"Are they coming round?" I ask Dad.

"YES, to discuss 'plans' for your granny and granddad's *fiftieth wedding anniversary*," Dad says.

I tell Dad my idea to go to a THEME PARK. Ha! Ha! He thinks I'm JOKING (I'm NOT!).

At least if the cousins are coming over too, Mum will bring out a few more hidden treats?

(I know where they all are.)

Found them!

Dad hangs up Mum's dress and
STARES at it.

"It looks a bit like a
HANDPRINT, doesn't it, Tom?"
he says.

"NO, not really," I say.

It's definitely time
to go to Derek's. The last thing Dad says to
me as I leave is:

Take a WARM coat. It's getting
colder and it's going to SNOW
later today.

"OK," I say, grabbing the first one
I can find.

Extra thin coat.

(It won't snow, I'll be fine.)

You're early, Derek says as he opens the door to me.

"I'm always early," I tell him. (I'm not.)

As we set off for school, a HUGE LORRY

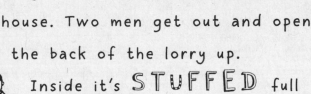

pulls up outside my other NEXT-DOOR NEIGHBOUR'S

house. Two men get out and open the back of the lorry up.

Inside it's STUFFED full of

boxes. "I wonder who's moving in?" Derek says.

"PLEASE not that girl who kept making those horrible faces at me.

She was even more annoying than Marcus."

"She must be BAD then," Derek laughs.

Mum is looking at the lorry through the window upstairs.

"Time to go. My mum's being nosy."

As we walk to school, Derek and I chat about what we did last night. (Blah blah **S**nakes and **L**adders blah blah Rooster ate my dinner.)

Then Derek says,

Rooster!

sausage

"It's getting really **COLD**, isn't it?"

It SO is.

I suggest doing *fast* walking to school.

"Let's go..."

We're the FIRST kids to arrive in school when it starts to **SNOW** just a bit. There's enough snow coming down to get **EXCITED** about, but not enough to make a PROPER snowball yet.

I try anyway by scraping up the snow around me.

Tiny snowball

The marks I've made on the ground have given me a very good idea. I find a nice stick so my hands don't get too cold and start scraping the snow.

"Hey, look at this..." I say to Derek.

"SNOW DOODLES!"

Doodling keeps me busy and stops me thinking about how COLD I am.

I wish I had on a thicker coat now.

By the time the bell goes for school, my SNOW DOODLES! have got MASSIVE.

Some little kids are watching me draw.

Marcus Meldrew turns up and wants to see what everyone's looking at.

He says, "Let me through, I'm a STAR PUPIL" and pushes in.

Oh, it's you, Tom. I thought there was something INTERESTING going on.

One little kid tells Marcus,

"He's really good at drawing."

"Thanks!" I reply.

Marcus scoffs and says, "He's OK."

The bell's gone for the start of school.
AMY PORTER walks past
me and I tell her,
"I got a bit carried away."
"I can see that," she says.
I do a few more lines on my doodle, then
follow Amy into school.
" Mr Fullerman is already writing
on the board when we get to class. He
says, **"HURRY UP and SIT DOWN, everyone,
you've all seen SNOW before."**
Someone at the back of the class says (I haven't.
Solid, Norman and Marcus Meldrew are looking
out of the window, along with a few
other kids too. Solid sits back down
and says to me, "Your snow doodle looks great
from the window, Tom. Not sure Mr Fullerman
will like it, though?"
Oh NO! I didn't think of THAT!

Maybe if I can keep Mr Fullerman AWAY from the window it might get COVERED UP by falling snow?

It's a good plan.

More kids want to look out of the window now, which is NOT helping.

Mr Fullerman turns to the whole class and says, **"No more STARING at the snow out of the window."**

I WISH he'd hurry up and START the lesson!

(That's not something I think very often.)

Mr Fullerman is GLARING at us all.

"Well, Class 5F, we have a very exciting week ahead. We're going to be inviting – NORMAN WATSON!"

Everyone starts laughing because Norman thinks he's been invited somewhere.

"Where am I going, SIR?"

"SIT DOWN, Norman."

Mr Fullerman starts walking towards the
WINDOW.

He's going to see my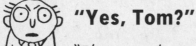

Quickly I jump up and say, "Mr Fullerman?"

 "Yes, Tom?"

"I'm wondering about the snow ... errr?"

I can't think what to say.

So I have a COUGHING fit, which kills a
bit more time.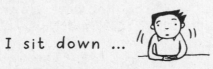

cough

cough

cough

 "Are you OK, Tom? Do you need some
water?"

"I've forgotten my question, sir."

"Sit down, then."

I sit down ...

then STAND back up again.

MARCUS puts up his hand.

"Tom has DRAWN pictures in the SNOW outside, sir. That's what we're all looking at."

THANKS a LOT, Marcus. ☹

Mr Fullerman walks over to the window and takes a lOOk outside.

(He's bound to see my doodle now.)

...I'm in trouble. There'll be

Doomed

 NO STAR PUPIL BADGE for me!

Mr Fullerman is STARING out of the window. Then at me. "You've been VERY busy, Tom."

(I have.) "Yes, sir."

"EVERYONE come and take a look at Tom's doodle, then sit back down."

HUH? REALLY? I peer out of the window and it's not as bad as I thought.

Luckily, Caretaker Stan (and the falling snow) have covered up some of the doodle. PHEW!

(Though Mrs Worthington still looks a bit dodgy.)

With all the SNOW stuff going on,
I've only just noticed the EXTRA DESK that's
appeared at the end of our row.

"Who's that desk for?"
I ask Amy. She doesn't know.

"Maybe the classroom is going to
be changed round again?" she suggests.
Mr Fullerman hasn't done that since he
moved me to the front of the class to stop
me from doodling.

(It worked ... a bit.)
I don't want AMY to move, as she helps me
with my work (even if she doesn't know it).

There is
ONE desk I
wouldn't mind moving...

My desk

FAR AWAY

MARCUS'S DESK

EXTRA HISTORY

Mr Fullerman reminds us that he'll be choosing **NEW STAR PUPILS** before the OPEN DAY, which is coming up soon.

(OPEN DAY is when new kids and parents come to look round the school.)

"AND a few of my class will be asked to be EXTRA HELPERS too," he adds.

"If you've NOT been a STAR PUPIL before and you've given in your homework on time, you might get the chance to be one THIS time," he tells us. Homework

I'd LOVE that. **STAR PUPILS** get to stay in the LIBRARY some lunchtimes too.

Especially good in WINTER if you've forgotten to bring a WARM coat (like I have).

Shiver
Shiver

Mr Fullerman hands round today's worksheets on VIKINGS.

"Take out your HISTORY BOOKS, please."

(What history book?

I must have left mine at home.)

I find a few spare sheets of paper in my bag to write on, which means I don't have to tell Mr Fullerman I've forgotten my book.

rummage

Shame

LACK OF HISTORY BOOK + SPARE PAPER = NO STAR PUPIL BADGE

I must remember to STICK the bits of paper into my HISTORY book so they don't get lost.

(It's a good plan.)

Wrinkly Paper

Our class has been learning all about the VIKINGS. Last week we read some Good STUFF about

VIKING  L O N G boats and how they used them to **INVADE** different countries.

VIKINGS were **FIERCE!**

Mr Fullerman starts drawing something on the whiteboard, which always gets my attention.

Mmmmmm, not sure what it is yet.
It could be a VIKING HELMET?

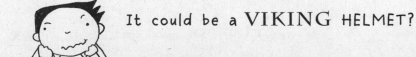

He turns round and says,

No one knows for sure if the VIKINGS REALLY did wear helmets that looked like this with REAL animal horns sticking out.

I'm REALLY TRYING to pay attention to Mr Fullerman. But it's SO hard when all I can see is this...

Ha! Ha! Ha! Ha!

Ha! Ha! Ha! Ha!

The WHOLE class have noticed now...

Florence Mitchell puts up her hand and tells Mr Fullerman what we're laughing at. **"OK, very funny, 5F."** Mr Fullerman smiles and moves away from the board.

(I'm still laughing.)

The lesson this morning has been SO good that (surprisingly for me) I've managed to forget about the SNOW and IGNORE Marcus completely. Which is not always easy

Groan

to do. I spoke too soon.

Marcus is *NUDGING* me.

"Guess what?"

"What, Marcus?"

"I don't think you're getting a ★ BADGE this time, Tom."

"How do you know? I might."

"Your name's not on Mr Fullerman's list."

(He's SO nosy.)

"You could be wrong, Marcus. It's not like you've never been wrong before."

Then he starts going on about his (badge) again.

With my **STAR PUPIL BADGE** on, kids in the other classes know that I'm EXTRA smart.

"Lucky you, Marcus," I say, sighing.

I wasn't expecting to be a **STAR PUPIL** yet because most of my homework has either been late or a tiny bit CRUNCHED up (sometimes it's been both).

My last piece of homework got STUCK to a doodle drawing that I threw away.

When I finally found it in the bin it was VERY CRINKLED.

I TRIED to *SMOOTH* it out, then stuck it into my book and put it under something heavy to keep it flat.

my book

But it didn't work.

I had to give my homework in anyway – Mr Fullerman wasn't THAT impressed.

(At least I did it ... that's something.)

VIKING
Homework
Tom Gates

Here are some INTERESTING things
about Vikings.

1. They were VERY good at making and

sailing longboats.

2. They used to grow a LOT of

vegetables like CABBAGES (which I hate).

3. Vikings made houses from wood

and they sometimes put TURF or grass

on the roof. I think my dad should

do that to his shed (I might try it).

4. Vikings did a LOT of weaving. (I think.)

Tom,
No more wrinkled homework
like this.
Mr Fullerman

AN EXTRA SNOWY BREAK TIME

Mr Fullerman is TELLING us all to **"be CAREFUL outside. The school will NOT be closing just because there's a tiny bit of snow."**

The whole class go AWWWWWWWWWW.

Unless, of course, the snow gets a LOT WORSE.

YEEEEEAAAAHHHHH!

We all cheer.

"The ground is slippery, so NO running OR snowball fights at break time. We don't want a repeat of what happened to Mr Keen last year, do we?"

"NO, Mr Fullerman," we all say.

Our headmaster, Mr Keen, got CAUGHT up in a BIG school SNOWBALL FIGHT. (He stepped out of the door JUST at the wrong time.)

We only realized Mr Keen was SO CROSS when the snow started to MELT off his REALLY **HOT RED FACE.**

"BE sensible!" YES, SIR!

As soon as we see snow everyone goes NUTS.

Caretaker Stan is throwing special GRIT and salt down everywhere to make it less slippy. Mrs Mumble and Mr Sprocket are on break-time duty and are being very careful not to slip too.

I'm beginning to wish I'd worn a warmer coat. Who knew it was going to snow?
(Apart from Dad.)

Take a warm coat. It's going to snow

I'm starting to SHIVER and get chilly.

"I'm NOT cold at all,"

Norman says.

That's because he never stays still for very

long. He's scooping  up snow from the

wall to make snowballs.

I join in and try to forget about

the cold by making ... let me see.

A mini snowman.

This bit of bendy wire is PERFECT for the hair.

It doesn't take long for

Norman to guess who it is.

Ha! Ha! Ha!

My hands (" ") have gone a bit numb from

holding the snow (I'm not wearing my mittens).

I start waving them around

to warm them up.

Derek says, "I know, let's play Rock Scissors Paper to keep our hands warm."
(Which is a good idea.) It's an EASY and QUICK
game to play.
We're getting ready
like THIS...

One Two Three...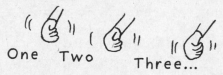
Then we make different shapes with our hands.

Rock wins.

When Marcus comes over and says,

What are you doing?

"Playing Rock Scissors Paper.
Want to play?" Solid asks.
Marcus says, "OK."
We gather round in a circle, then go ...

... ready.

One Two Three...

Paper over Rock.

Scissors break on Rock.

Scissors cut Paper.

We're all looking at Marcus, who's doing

something different with his hand.

"I win!" he tells us. "How do you

work that out, Marcus?" I ask.

His hand is making a WOBBLY wavy movement.

"What's THAT?"

Derek asks.

"It's WATER -

Water wins over Rock, Scissors and Paper."

"Water?" we all say. "I've never seen

WATER in this game before," Solid says.

"Well I have. That's the way I play it.

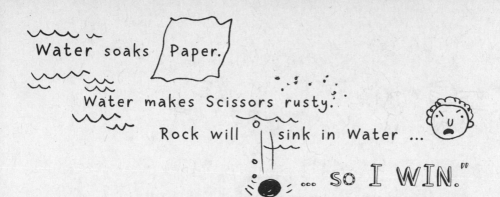

Water soaks Paper.

Water makes Scissors rusty.

Rock will sink in Water ...

... so I WIN."

We all l⊙⊙k at each other and roll our eyes.

"Let's get on with the next game," Derek says. So we do.

But Marcus does it AGAIN!

"Water - I win."

"Hang on, does anything beat Water?" I want to know.

"If you keep on doing WATER all the time you'll just keep winning," Solid tells Marcus.

"So? You can do it too."

"Then no one will win," Solid points out.

"Let's have ANOTHER game then,"
I suggest.
Norman does **ROCK** too early so we
have to start again. I'm going to do something
different next time. Here goes. READY.

One
Two
Three... Norman does - Rock.
Solid - Paper. Derek - Scissors.
Marcus does his stupid wavy hand thing and I
make a STARBURST shape with my hand.
"I WIN!" I say.

"What's THAT?" Marcus wants to know.
"It's SUNSHINE - look, see-"
I do it some more.

"SUN - BURNS PAPER melts metal and turns stones to
...DUST...

And dries out all the water — 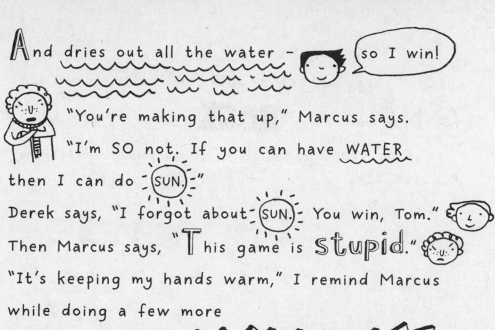 so I win!

"You're making that up," Marcus says.

"I'm SO not. If you can have WATER then I can do SUN."

Derek says, "I forgot about SUN. You win, Tom."

Then Marcus says, "This game is stupid."

"It's keeping my hands warm," I remind Marcus while doing a few more

HAND STARBURSTS.

(Marcus is getting annoyed.)

He says, "As I'm a **STAR PUPIL**, I can go and keep warm in the library while you LOT have to stay out here playing stupid games in the COLD.

← Marcus being warm

Solid tells us,

"I'm going to get a **STAR PUPIL BADGE** too,

Mr Fullerman told me."

"Well done, Solid," I say.

Derek asks, "Do you have to go to the

OPEN DAY, then?"

Before he can answer, Marcus **BUTTS**

in and says, "Well I'M going to the

OPEN DAY." (Marcus is trying to look important.)

Solid adds, "I have to show people around the

school as well."

Solid will make a very good **STAR PUPIL**

because he's nice and helpful.

(Unlike someone else I know.)

It's started to **SNOW** A LOT MORE NOW.

Mrs Mumble blows her whistle.

"Break time's over! Be careful going inside,"

she says just as Mr Sprocket

SKIDS past her.

Norman makes a few more snowballs, then leaves them in a pile.

I'm following Derek and Solid with a crowd of kids back into the school when I feel something COLD and WET on my NECK.

"What's that?"

I reach behind and SOMEONE'S put a BIG SLUSHY snowball in my HOOD! YUCK. "Who did that?"

Derek says he didn't see who it was.

It wasn't Solid, who's in front of me. I turn round and STARE at the kids behind me.

ONE face stands out in the crowd.

"Wasn't me," Marcus says, trying to be convincing.

(He's not.)

85

I take the snow out of my hood. It has already turned into SNOW MUSH.

I check that no one's watching. I don't want to get into trouble with any eagle-eyed teachers.

Then I LOB the SNOW MUSH UP in the air towards Marcus.

I quickly turn round and RUN to my class before it lands.

I'm listening out for a nice BIG SPLAT noise, which should be right about NOW?

...Still listening ...

nothing yet.

Then I hear ...

"Who THREW that SNOWBALL?"

I'm not sure HOW I managed to hit Mr Keen, but I make sure I get back to my desk and sit down ════════ *F A S T.*

(Lucky escape.)

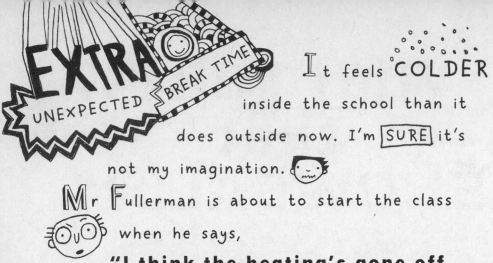

EXTRA UNEXPECTED BREAK TIME

It feels **COLDER** inside the school than it does outside now. I'm SURE it's not my imagination.

Mr Fullerman is about to start the class when he says,

"I think the heating's gone off. That's not good."

He tells us this just as Mrs Mumble interrupts him with an **EMERGENCY ANNOUNCEMENT** over the LOUDspeaker.

"Hello, everyone."

"Hello, Mrs Mumble," we all say back.

(Which is a bit odd when Mrs Mumble's not even in the same room.)

"You might have noticed it's got a LOT colder in the school. We're having a few problems with the heating.

Our wonderful caretaker Stan is trying his best to fix it, but if the snow gets any worse, we'll have to crackle CRACK m ... u m ... bl ... e i ... sk du ... g ... h ... o ... a'eb ... p iq k w ... u."

Huh? What did Mrs Mumble say? Mr Fullerman can't hear either. I think she said something GOOD because kids are cheering in the other classrooms. Mr Fullerman suggests we put our coats back on to keep WARM. But my coat's a bit damp (especially the hood) so I don't bother.

The SNOW is falling even faster now, with BIG flakes, making the school grounds look clean and white (for a change).

Next door, Mr Sprocket is taking his class to the hall.

"We might have to leave school early today. We're going to wait in the hall, as it's warmer there," he tells Mr Fullerman so he knows what's going on.

Mr Fullerman thinks it's a good idea to follow them too. Norman's jumping **UP** and **down** and the kids in class are already getting excited. SNOW BREAK

All I heard was Mr Sprocket saying, LEAVE SCHOOL EARLY. I didn't hear anything else after that.

AMY always knows what's happening so I follow her.

Norman is causing **CHAOS** by pretending to throw non-existent snowballs at everyone until Mr Fullerman stops him.

ENOUGH

We head to the hall. Caretaker Stan has turned on some EMERGENCY HEATERS, which are working nicely.

Mr Fullerman says we should get out our reading books and sit quietly while we're waiting. 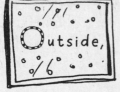 (Which is another thing I've forgotten. Groan.)

Most of the school is STUFFED into the hall so it's almost TOO WARM now. heat heat heat

Outside, the snow is REALLY coming down thick and FAST when Mr Keen joins us and gets our attention.

"I have some BAD NEWS," he says.

S I L E N C E...

"Unfortunately, the school will have to close until the heating is fixed."

HOORRAAYY!

Looking at all the happy faces of the kids (and teachers), Mr Keen is the only person who thinks it's **BAD** news.

My class are all *BUZZING* with plans to play in the snow. We'll have loads of time to go *SLEDGING* if the school's going to be closed for a while.

WHICH is going to be **AMAZING.**

Mr Fullerman tells our class we can't go home straight away.

AWWWWWWWWWWW!

"The school office has to contact everyone's homes to make sure you can all get back safely."

Which all sounds very OFFICIAL.

Mrs Nap wants to know,

"Hands up, who wants to come to choir practice early? Anyone?"

(No hands – which is a bit awkward.)

Mrs Mumble has a list of kids who are allowed to go home now, and another list of kids who have to wait to be collected. OBVIOUSLY I'll be allowed to go home NOW, because I live SO close. I'm listening out for my name...

Which doesn't get called.

I have to wait for my dad to come and pick me up, which is `annoying`. 🙁 Shame →

At least Derek said he'd wait with me so I won't be waiting on my own. We only live down the road so Dad will get here QUICKLY I'm sure (I hope so).

Wrong shoes ←

My school →

SLIP

Fifteen minutes later

Marcus is standing by the heater and **HOGGING** ALL the warmth.

"I'm allowed to because I have a **STAR PUPIL BADGE**," he says, which is **NOT** TRUE.

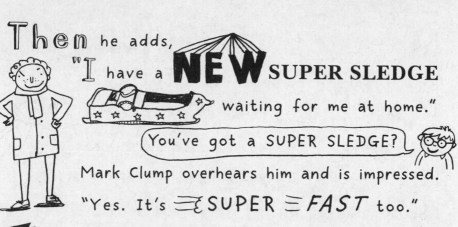

Then he adds, "I have a **NEW** SUPER SLEDGE waiting for me at home."

You've got a SUPER SLEDGE?

Mark Clump overhears him and is impressed.

"Yes. It's SUPER *FAST* too."

"Bring it to the park tomorrow and show us," I suggest.

Then Solid comes over and says BYE and that he'll see us at the park tomorrow. He's going back to Mark Clump's house.

Marcus says, "I'm GOING STRAIGHT home."

Good for you, Marcus. ☺

"I wouldn't want to get SNOWED in at someone else's HOUSE. That would be a NIGHTMARE," he says.

"Who for?" I wonder.

Marcus did visit my house AGES ago. And I've been to his house, but only by accident. THIS IS WHAT HAPPENED:

I was in the same class as Marcus in little school and HIS mum asked my mum if I'd like to play at his house after school?

My mum said, He'd love to. I didn't really have a choice. Mum took me to see Marcus the next day and he OPENED the front door and JUST STARED at me like I was a MARTIAN. Then he SHOUTED,

MUM ... NOT THIS TOM! I wanted the *other* Tom to come over. He's the WRONG TOM!

I didn't even know there was another boy called Tom in our school? Neither did Marcus's mum, apparently. In the end Marcus said he'd "MAKE DO" with me.

"You might as well come in."

Which wasn't exactly a good start to our ☆FUN☆ play date. His mum was really sorry about getting the "TWO Toms" mixed up. She was EXTRA nice to me and kept reminding Marcus that I was his guest.

humph

"Marcus, let TOM choose first - he's your guest."

"Thanks, Mrs Meldrew. I choose THIS cake."

It drove Marcus CRAZY. I enjoyed myself a LOT more than I thought I was going to.

Marcus is annoyed because he has to wait for Mrs Mumble to call his parents. **"I** want to get **HOME** and play on my **SUPER SLEDGE."**

(My dad is taking AGES to pick us up too.)

Most of the other kids have left the school now. We're some of the last ones still here.

Oh, and Caretaker Stan, who looks more stressed out than usual. He keeps on going up and down the hall frowning while holding different-sized spanners. **N**ow he's holding ...

... a feather duster?

"It's a long story," he says to

Mr Fullerman.

 Feather DUSTER + Broken boiler = STILL NOT MENDED

Brad's uncle has just turned up, which only leaves us. (WHY am I ALWAYS the last one to be picked up from school?*) "Are you sure your dad is coming for you?" Derek asks.

"YES, I'm sure." (I'm [not] totally sure.)

Eventually my dad turns up wearing some WEIRD snow boots and something on his head I think Granny Mavis knitted him.

"AT LAST!" I tell him, putting on my (damp) thin coat.

*See page 222, Tom Gates Is Absolutely Fantastic (At Some Things).

99

"We'd better get going. The SNOW is getting VERY heavy out there," Dad says. Mrs Mumble runs up to talk to Mr Fullerman and Marcus.

Marcus, your parents have just called. They're stuck on a train in the snow and could be a while. As the school will be closing soon, it's best that you go home with Tom, if that's all right with you, Mr Gates?

Dad says it's fine and I'm speechless. "OK, Marcus. They'll pick you up as soon as they can," Mrs Mumble assures him. I'm not sure who looks more fed up, ME huh? - or Marcus. I can't believe he's got to come to MY house!

Derek thinks it's funny. "You might get snowed in!" he says. "Stuck with Marcus for DAYS and DAYS! Imagine that." He laughs.

(I'm trying not to.)

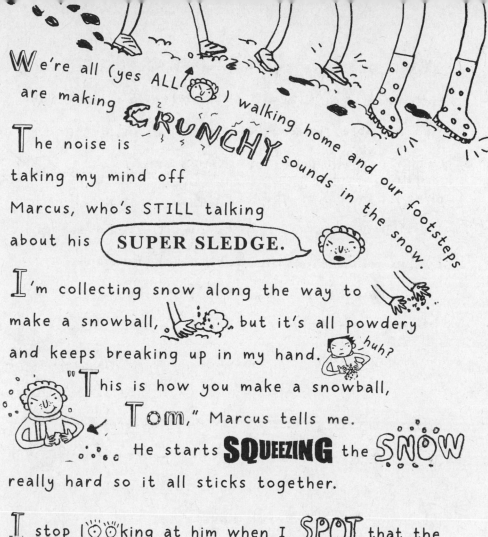

We're all (yes ALL) walking home and our footsteps are making CRUNCHY sounds in the snow.

The noise is taking my mind off Marcus, who's STILL talking about his SUPER SLEDGE.

I'm collecting snow along the way to make a snowball, but it's all powdery and keeps breaking up in my hand. huh?

"This is how you make a snowball, Tom," Marcus tells me. He starts SQUEEZING the SNOW really hard so it all sticks together.

I stop looking at him when I SPOT that the LORRY from this morning is STILL outside the neighbours' house. Dad says, "They moved in, but the lorry got stuck." (Oh great, NEW neighbours AND Marcus.)

I ask Dad who the new neighbours are. Dad tells me, "You'll meet them soon, I'm sure." Marcus sees the snowball in my hand. "You'd better NOT throw that at me, I'm your GUEST." sigh

Then Dad says, "Don't throw it at me either ... I'm your dad!" as he goes into the house.

(It's tempting ... but I resist.)

Derek throws his snowball at a small tree, which makes all the snow fall from the branches.

"NICE SHOT!" I say and Derek says, "Let's meet up tomorrow - and good luck today!"

"Thanks, Derek," I say (I'll need it with Marcus).

I decide to **CHUCK** my snowball at the side of the lorry. There's a nice **big "O"** on the side so I AIM for that.

The snowball makes a nice **DUFFF** sound.

REMOVAL
VAN LTD

And that's when I realize ...

SOMEONE'S INSIDE! Oh! Oh! Time to go.

I run to the front door when MARCUS decides to *LOB* a snowball

at **ME!** I duck and the snowball *FLIES* OVER ...

... my head and into the BOX the man is holding.

"WHO THREW THAT?"

THIS WAY UP

(That would be Marcus – but he's nowhere to be seen.) I don't want to hang around. So I *quickly* run into the house and shut the door.

Inside, Marcus tells me,

"THAT was all your fault."

"How do you work that one out, Marcus?" I wonder.

"You shouldn't have ducked," he tells me.

(I really hope his mum and dad don't take too long to come and get him ... groan.)

EXTRA ANNOYING

Marcus is only here for a few hours before his dad comes to get him. ☺

Which is a RELIEF.

In that time he STILL manages to:

- Get me into trouble with the new neighbours.

THIS WAY UP

WHO THREW THAT?

- EAT MY LAST caramel wafer.

- **Mess up** my copies of **ROCK WEEKLY**.

OOPS!

- Break a STRING on my guitar.

- READ the FAN letter I was planning to send to **DUDE 3** (the best band in the WORLD).

- Draw a **stupid** picture of me on MY doodle wall.

The worst thing is his drawing makes Delia laugh. She thinks it's "HILARIOUS", which only encourages him to keep drawing.

Ha! Ha! Ha!

Ha Ha!

"That looks just like Tom. You're really good at drawing, Marcus," she tells him.

(It doesn't look anything like me.)

I can't WAIT for Marcus to leave. When his parents finally arrive, he complains that they took too long. I only RELAX as I watch him walk out of the door. "SIGH" But that

doesn't last for very long, as the doorbell goes again.

Ding dong

This time it's Uncle Kevin, Aunty Alice and the cousins. I'd forgotten they were coming round. Dad had forgotten too. He hasn't told Mum either. She is VERY surprised to see ⊙⊙ them all standing in the hallway.

And EVEN MORE surprised they have suitcases.

Are you all moving in?

Mum JOKES as they take off coats.

Aunty Alice says, "It's SO kind of you, Rita. I don't know what we would have done otherwise." (Mum looks puzzled.)

"It was TERRIBLE," Uncle Kevin continues.

"One bit of snow and we've suddenly got NO heating or HOT WATER. The water pipes are FROZEN and all the HOTELS near us are fully booked."

(107)

Aunty Alice puts her hand to her head like it's the WORST thing ever.

Mum suddenly gets that they ARE STAYING.

She says, OH ... I see.

Uncle Kevin reminds Dad, "We'd already arranged with Frank to come over today, so it seemed the most sensible thing to do, with the weather being so bad."

Mum says, "Frank didn't mention that."

Dad pretends to look confused.

"We can always sleep in the shed?" Uncle Kevin suggests, though I'm not sure he really means it.

Aunty Alice doesn't look too keen but I wouldn't mind. I say,

I'll sleep in the shed!

Nobody takes any notice.

Mum tells Uncle Kevin not to be silly. "You can have the sofa bed. It's very comfy."

 Uncle Kevin annoys Mum by saying, "We'll be fine roughing it here for a bit."

"That's good of you," Dad replies through gritted TEETH.

Mum tells the cousins that they can sleep in my room. WHERE? HOW?

This is the size of my room.

And this is the size of the cousins.

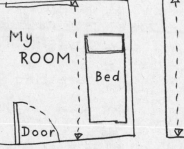

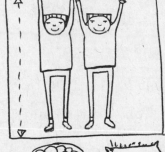

ADD a few other things

too and the whole room is

I'll sleep in the shed, I say again.

"No one is sleeping in MY shed," Dad says, being very protective. Mum tells Dad to call **THE FOSSILS** and make sure they're OK too. They are FINE and wondering what all the fuss is about. Granny Mavis says,

"It's just SNOW. I've been very busy

knitting and have posted off some WARM KNITS for EVERYONE." Which sounds interesting.

When Delia emerges from her room, she gets a bit of a surprise. "We've got a full house tonight!" Mum tells her.

The only thing Delia says is

Don't go near my room.

(Which I take as a challenge!)

After everyone has settled in, the "grown-ups" go into the kitchen to "CHAT" about **THE FOSSILS'** ⭐*50*ᵀᴴ⭐ *wedding anniversary.*

Me and the cousins go and watch some TV. I'm flicking through the channels and there's loads of news about

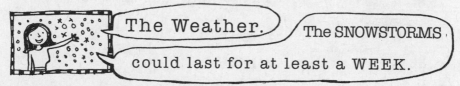

The Weather. The SNOWSTORMS could last for at least a WEEK.

A WEEK! If the cousins have to stay in our house for a WHOLE WEEK, we'll run out of food, I think.

Yum yum

EMPTY

I can hear the wind outside, which is really strong and making the snow swirl around. Then suddenly the TV picture goes all

 FUZZY, then disappears completely.

"THE TV'S GONE OFF!" the cousins both shout in a **PANIC!**

It's the bad weather interfering with the signal, Dad shouts from the kitchen.

Uncle Kevin ignores Dad and comes over to the TV. He starts fiddling with all the buttons, pressing everything.

Then he turns it **ON** and **OFF** again. That doesn't work either.

BLANK

"It's the bad weather interfering with the signal." Uncle Kevin repeats exactly what Dad already said.

As the TV'S [not] working, I ask the cousins if they want to listen to some **DUDE 3** and play some music?

Can we play it **EXTRA** loud? they want to know.

"Why not, if you want to,"  I say.

"**YEAH, LET'S!**"

I think it's a good idea because **LOUD music**

really annoys Delia.

Ha! Ha!

EXTRA NOISY Neighbours

KNOCK
KNOCK
KNOCK

(Apparently, Delia isn't the only

person our **loud music** really annoys.)

KNOCK

KNOCK

KNOCK

It's coming from next

door's wall.

We knock back a few

times before it stops.

Then our doorbell rings.

- Ring
- ring
- I can hear my mum saying, "OH...? I'm so sorry. We can't hear much noise from the kitchen. I'll let them know." One of the new neighbours has just asked Mum if we wouldn't mind turning down the music.

Mum comes upstairs and stops us with a BIG Ssshhhh!

We aren't THAT loud!

"Let's not get off to a bad start with the new neighbours, shall we?"

(I've already done that.)

We quieten down a bit, but still manage to annoy Delia with a few versions of "DELIA'S A WEIRDO".

Delia's a WEIRDO

Bang!
Bang!

(Her favourite song - not.)

Dad's busy in the kitchen, seeing what we can eat for dinner. He says, Leftovers, I think. Some leftovers are better than others.

Leftover spaghetti bolognese ☺ = **DOUBLE YUM**

Leftover vegetable pie = **DOUBLE YUCK!** ☹

Mum hides vegetables that I don't like in pies. She thinks I won't notice.

parsnip

I always do.

Dad says, "Looks like it's leftover spaghetti, then."

Dad got confused about how much to cook and there's MASSES of it everywhere.

The cousins tell me they've brought their own snacks, which is one reason I don't mind them staying in my room.

But that doesn't stop them from **Chomping** up ALL the SPECIAL GUEST TREATS that Mum left out. I grab some for myself before they're all gone.

After dinner, Mum **SQUEEZES** the blow-up mattress and sleeping bags into the corner of my room. (It's the mattress we take camping - so it's hardly ever been used.)

Mum says we'll be "nice and snug".

I think she really means "CRAMPED". Dad couldn't find the foot pump and went RED in the face trying to **BLOW UP** the bed himself.

Uncle Kevin kept patting him on the head and saying, "Keep going, Frank - you can do it."

(Dad managed to look annoyed and puffed out at the same time.)

Next **M**um goes downstairs to make up the sofa bed for Aunty Alice and Uncle Kevin, when suddenly they appear wearing matching pyjamas, slippers and dressing gowns.

Delia walks in and says,

Oh my,

then goes in the kitchen.

"We don't want to put you to any trouble, Rita," **A**unty Alice tells **M**um.

"It's no trouble at all," she says, followed by, "WOW, don't you both look so ... MATCHING!"

"We're the same colour as FRANK'S face after blowing up that mattress." **A**unty Alice and Uncle Kevin **LAUGH** at their joke.

Ha! Ha! Ha!

(Dad can hear them from the kitchen and he's not laughing.)

Then Uncle Kevin says, "We should all wear coordinating clothes for this FAMILY PORTRAIT. It will look **SO** MUCH better."

"What family portrait?" Delia asks.

"For your grandparents' fiftieth anniversary," Mum says.

"Do we have to wear pyjamas?" I want to know.

"NO WAY am I doing a FAMILY PORTRAIT," Delia tells everyone.

 Aunty Alice says, "It'll be **FUN!**"

"It's **NOT** my idea of FUN," Delia mutters.

"How about a surprise party?" Mum suggests. Everyone likes that idea. ☺

"We'll have to keep it a secret or it won't work. No one can say a word – ESPECIALLY you, Tom."

Why me? I'm REALLY good at keeping secrets, I say.

"Are you, Tom?" Mum laughs.

Like it's news to her. So I REMIND her about some secrets I HAVE kept. Secrets LIKE:

* NOT telling Mr Fullerman that during Parents' Evening, they weren't actually sick, they just forgot it was on.

Dear Mr Fullerman
I'm sorry we couldn't come to Parents' Evening, we were both feeling very sick.
Yours sincerely
Mr and Mrs Gates

* How the VASE over there isn't really the one Uncle Kevin and Aunty Alice gave them because they broke it.

(I've not finished yet!)

* Mum doesn't really like the perfume Dad buys all the time. So she keeps it all in a drawer.

SEE! I told you I can keep secrets!

I think I've made my point.

Dad wants to know more about the perfume now.

"Never mind about that! What do Bob and Mavis really **NEED**?" Mum says (to avoid talking about the perfume).

I suggest they need new teeth — especially Granddad.

Which is true but not much of a present.

Then **DELIA JOINS IN**, which is a surprise. No one knew she was listening.

They need a new mobility scooter.

It's a great idea! Their one is pretty old and **ANCIENT**. (a bit like **THE FOSSILS**).

"It could be a joint present from everyone at the LEAFY GREEN OLD FOLKS' HOME and all of us too," Mum says.

So that's sorted then. **THE FOSSILS** are getting a **PARTY**, a mobility scooter ...

oh, and the FAMILY PORTRAIT. Lucky them.

Groan.

EXTRA GAMES

As the [TV] is still not working, I spend some time watching the ∴SNOW∴ get thicker. Then I ask the cousins if they want to play cards? ♠ (Granddad's been teaching me.)

The only game we all know is ∴SNAP∴ But it gets a bit NOISY and the cousins

keep arguing. So Uncle Kevin suggests we should have a game of charades instead. Which is a game we normally play at Christmas. Delia says "I'm Off" straight away. But everyone else seems keen. Especially Dad. He goes first, and mimes, "It's a film." "One word." "The WHOLE thing." It doesn't take long to guess it's

SUPERMAN.

Tea towel

Mum goes next.

My turn (I was very good).

Her mime is the whole thing.

(Tea towel again)

Answer: The Sound of Music

Imagine the cushion is a cub...

Answer: The Lion King

Aunty Alice doesn't want to have a go.

I can't think

The cousins do a simple mime.

Answer: Twins

NO one gets what Uncle Kevin is doing.

Jungle Book

Snakes on a Plane

Nope ... still no one gets it.

In the end he has to tell us what it was.

Who doesn't know The Elephant Man?

Eerrrr, me?

Mum suggests that we head off to bed - only she mimes it. ZZZZ)) I'm pretty tired now, so I don't mind going. Though it takes me **AGES** to get to sleep - mainly **because**:

1. The cousins keep bringing out nice things to eat.

2. The blow-up bed makes LOUD squeaky noises every time they move.

3. Aunty Alice snores so LOUDly I can hear it upstairs.

4. Uncle Kevin's snoring is even LOUDER. He sounds like a dinosaur.

5. I had to get up and go downstairs to check that it WASN'T a REAL **DINOSAUR**.

SNOOOOORRE

How is it even possible that you can be asleep and snore THAT LOUDLY?

I thought Mum and Dad were bad.

(They are quite bad.)

NEW NEIGHBOUR ALERT!

In the morning I jump out of bed and forget the COUSINS are in my room. I only just manage not to STEP on them.

They aren't properly awake or ready to move yet. So I grab some clothes and go to the bathroom BEFORE anyone else gets there.

Then I l○○k out of the window.

There's **SNOW** everywhere. It's all sparkly and white.

But the BIGGEST shock of all is ... someone's already in next door's garden.

OH! NO!

(125)

THERE'S THAT GIRL!

The one who pulled all those stupid faces at me.

Stupid face

She's making a SNOWMAN.

She IS my
new neighbour
then.

GROAN.

I don't want her to see me so I duck behind
the curtain. I have to go and tell Derek the
new-neighbour news NOW! I'm brushing
my teeth quickly (and being good) when a
snowball *ZOOMS* over our fence and into

Derek's garden.

WHHHOOOSSHHHHHH.

There goes another one. That girl's CHUCKING snowballs right into Derek's garden!

I have to warn Derek! I get dressed quickly, then run downstairs.

Aunty Alice and Uncle Kevin are AWAKE and in the kitchen already. Uncle Kevin is complaining about having a sore back. "That sofa bed was SO uncomfortable, I was awake ALL night," he says. (He wasn't the ONLY one.) I bet Uncle Kevin got a lot more sleep than anyone else did.

I don't say that though.

I say, "Morning! I'm going out in the snow - everyone's still asleep." Then I rush past to find my snow boots and a WARM coat. (This time.)

I haven't got any gloves, just a pair of mittens that Granny Mavis knitted for me last year – which are a bit sad. I ONLY wear them in emergencies – like now.

Sad mittens

Mum and Dad come downstairs and they look REALLY tired as well. Dad whispers to me, "Did you hear those two snoring last night?"

I nod.

"I thought I was bad," he says.

"You are," Mum tells him.

I can hear Derek in his garden with Rooster, who's barking A LOT. It must be the first time Rooster has seen snow?

Woof
woof

Woof
woof

Outside the snow is quite thick and I'm sinking in trying not to fall down. I call out to get his attention.

Derek! Derek!

Derek looks up, so I whisper, "IT'S HER! It's THAT girl – she's the new neighbour!"

When suddenly Derek has to duck

down because

another snowball FLIES over the fence.

"We know you're THERE – don't throw any more snowballs!" I shout.

"Or we'll chuck them BACK at you," Derek adds.

She keeps quiet, but we can see the top of her head behind the fence.

"Watch this," I tell Derek, who has to keep pulling Rooster out of the snow.

stuck → I make a really good snowball and aim it at the fence.

Wearing these stupid MITTENS makes it a LOT harder to throw the snowball in the RIGHT direction, though.

I do my *BEST* but the snowball flies OVER the fence and CRASHES right into THEIR KITCHEN WINDOW! Luckily it doesn't break.

OH! OH!

But there's a big SNOW SPLODGE on the outside.

Derek hides behind a wall while I try to FLATTEN myself against their fence so they won't see me.

I can hear the girl telling her dad what happened. She says, "It was that boy next door."

(That will be me then.)

"He's still there." (I wish I wasn't!)

I'm trying to edge my way back to the house without making the snow **crunch.** `crunch` `crunch` Which isn't EASY.

SLOWLY does it...

NEARLY ... there

when I feel someone tapping me on my head.

"Did you throw that snowball?"

I look up and they're both STARING down at me.

I say, "I'm sorry, it was an accident."

Which is *sort* of true.

I can't get back in the house fast enough. (Shame.)

Derek comes straight round and wants to know "what happened?"

"I got caught," I tell him.

Rooster is desperate to go out in the snow again.

Mum says, "Hello, Derek. Let Rooster go out in the garden if he wants." Then she wonders if Derek's met our new neighbours yet? "We have," he says.

"They seem nice, don't they?" Mum adds.

"Well, I'm NOT so sure," I mutter. Then Mum brings out a NEW HOME CARD.

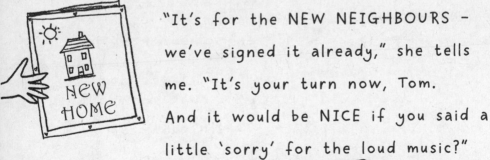

"It's for the NEW NEIGHBOURS - we've signed it already," she tells me. "It's your turn now, Tom. And it would be NICE if you said a little 'sorry' for the loud music?"

"Do I HAVE to?" I ask. (From the look Mum gives me, it's a stupid question, really.) I draw a monster and sign the card.

> Sorry for the loud music.
> From Tom

> Congratulations on your New Home.
>
> Love from the Gates family (next door), Rita, Frank, Tom and Delia x

The cousins are awake now and they're both watching me sign the card. "Can we sign it too?" they ask Mum. "Of course," she says. The cousins sign the card and add a bit EXTRA too. Mum puts the card in an envelope without reading it. (Which is a BIG mistake for both of us.)

> I'm NOT
> Sorry for the loud music.
> I'm going to do it again.
> From Tom
>
> Ha! Ha!

> Congratulations on your New Home.
>
> Love from the Gates family (next door), Rita, Frank, Tom and Delia x
>
> From the Gates cousins

EXTRA SPECIAL KNITTING

IT'S OFFICIAL – there's DEFINITELY NO SCHOOL TODAY or tomorrow if the heating doesn't get fixed. (Fingers crossed.) I do a little celebratory AIR PUNCH before I notice the cousins have scoffed all the breakfast that Mum's put out.

And I mean EVERYTHING.

Empty

Empty

Empty Empty

Empty

Empty

Nearly gone

Uncle Kevin is on the phone trying to get someone to fix their water pipes and heating.

He's NOT happy and  SHOUTING,

What do you mean you can't fix it for a WEEK!

 Mum and Dad aren't happy

about that either.

We still manage to get some post today,

which is surprising as it's so snowy.

 The postman says, "Luckily for

me your parcel wasn't heavy."

I open it up and PEER inside.

It's from THE FOSSILS. Looks like

Granny Mavis has been knitting a LOT.

She's made something for EVERYONE.

So I hand out: knitted hats for Dad and Uncle

Kevin. Extra FLUFFY scarves for Aunty Alice,

Mum and Delia (who doesn't want to try it on).

    I got the same

as the cousins...

CAKE JUMPERS with cherry hats.

click

Granny's gone to a lot of trouble, but I don't think I'll be wearing this jumper or hat outside or ANYWHERE – not unless I want people to STARE at me. Like Delia is right now. Ha!
(Trust her to turn up with Mum's phone and take photos.)

"That's enough, Delia," I tell her. "I feel stupid."

"You look stupid," she tells me.

The cousins say the jumpers are making them feel hungry again. (How is that even possible?)

EXTRA special SNOW

Derek comes over so we can go sledging.
The cousins want to come too.
"We don't have a sledge, though," they say
(which is a problem). Then I remember I don't
have one EITHER. "What shall we use?"
I ask Derek, who says I can share his sledge.

(Which is nice of him.)

Mum has a suggestion.
"Take these tea trays and thick
plastic bags. That's what I used when I
was little."   Really?
We're going sledging, Mum, not shopping,
                                              I tell her.
"They work just as well - be careful and look
after your cousins, won't you?"
"Yes, Mum," I say (knowing THAT won't be easy).
We'll give the tea trays and bags a try even
though the cousins aren't keen.

Dad's decided he's coming with us because Uncle Kevin is driving him `NUTS`. Which is fine by me (he can look after the cousins). "Your Uncle Kevin's been complaining about everything," he tells me.

(It's TRUE, I've heard him.)

"None of your pens work."

"What's this coffee?" — Coffee

"This room needs a lick of paint." That's it! I'm off.

Dad's pleased to see we're all dressed warmly for the snow. (The cousins are still wearing their cherry hats.) I'm forced to wear those mittens again. Never mind, I'll keep my hands in my pockets.

warm coat

When we get to the park, the first person I see is AMY PORTER, who's with a few other girls from my class.

They wave at us so I wave back.

"Nice mittens, Tom," 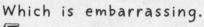 AMY says.

Which is embarrassing.

Florence tells us they've been

sledging already.

"We're making this ↓GIANT snowman

now," she adds. Which is pretty impressive. ☺

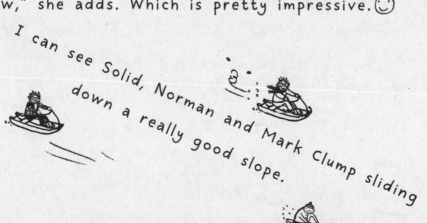

I can see Solid, Norman and Mark Clump sliding down a really good slope.

MARCUS MELDREW is there too, admiring his OWN **SUPER SLEDGE** and showing it off to anyone who looks at it.

It's MINE

It looks pretty *FLASH* compared to what we've got.

"Nice sledge, Marcus," Derek says.

"I **KNOW**, it's the **BEST**," Marcus says, looking at our tea trays and plastic bags. "Are you really using those?" he asks.

"Yes we are – what's the problem?" I ask him.

"Falling OFF? They don't look very safe. This sledge is super STURDY and fast. Watch this – I'll show you how it's done."

"**W**e're watching," I say wearily.

Marcus gets ready to go down the hill. Norman couldn't be bothered to wait for Marcus, who's fussing with the sledge. He goes down first.
WHHEEEEEEEEEEEEEEEEEEEEEEE.

Marcus tries to

set off next ...

only he doesn't move.

He shuffles along a bit more with his feet, trying to get it going. He's not sliding at all. "Stupid snow! It's TOO THICK.

Can someone give me a push?" he asks.

Derek and I both push him. Marcus starts to go

really ... really ... really ...

slowly... He has to

shuffle himself to the

bottom of the hill with his feet.

"More like SUPER SNAIL than SUPER
SLEDGE,"
I say to Derek.

Then it's our turn.

Surprisingly, our tea trays work REALLY well. **R**ooster LOVES sliding on the tray with Derek. His ears flap around a lot in the wind.

WHHEEEEEEEEEE!

Flappi ear

Marcus insists his sledge must be **broken** and that's why it wouldn't slide.

"What you need is a tea tray like ours," I tell him. (Which doesn't go down too well.) "I've had enough of sledging today, there are too many kids here getting in my way," Marcus says. Then he goes off in a HUFF to make a snowman.

I can see Dad chatting to some of the other parents and LAUGHING. So at least he's cheered up ☺ (which is good news).

The cousins have stopped sledging now because their feet have burst through their plastic bags. "Let's make a snowman," they say. (Good idea.)

I decide to make a **SNOW MONSTER,** which attracts a bit of attention.

Some kids come over to watch me.

"Nice monster," one says.

"And mittens," another adds.

"Thanks," I say. (I'd forgotten about those.)

Then **AMY** and Florence Mitchell turn up, so I say, "These mittens are EXCELLENT for smoothing down the snow."

(Like I planned to wear them all along.)

I'm about to put the finishing touches to my monster's head WHEN ...

WHACK

a snowball hits it and half of its **HEAD** falls off!

"WHAT! OH NO! That took me **AGES!**"

I say, l**oo**king round to see where it's come from?

I can see someone peering out from behind a tree. I get a handful of snow and make it into a snowball. Then I take AIM and throw it as far as

I can

at the TREE.

Which was **FULL** of snow on the branches.
Well, it [was] full of snow — until it all fell on
MARCUS.   (I guessed it was him.)

CLOSE UP

RESULT!

He looks a bit like a snowman himself now.
Derek congratulates me on my snowball throwing
while the cousins just say they're still (HUNGRY.)
Rooster's getting cold too. So we decide to
find Dad in case Marcus tries to throw any
more snowballs at us.   snow →

"Did you have fun?" Dad asks on the way home.
"I hope Uncle Kevin's heating is fixed. I can't take
any more **SNORING**," he whispers to me.

Derek takes Rooster home, as he's very tired from playing in the snow.

When we walk into our house, Mum looks very HAPPY (which is a good sign).

She tells the cousins, "Everything's fixed so you'll be able to go home today. I bet you're pleased about that?"

(Not as pleased as Dad is!)

Mum's also smiling because she's found out my school is open again tomorrow as well.

GROAN.

SLEEP!
Yeah

The cousins and Aunty Alice go and pack up their stuff before Uncle Kevin comes back to pick them up.

dump

When he arrives, he announces,

"I've managed to SORT everything out as usual. Let's go back home to a bit of luxury."

Which doesn't go down too well with Mum.

Charming

I can see Dad rolling his EYES 👁 👁 behind Uncle Kevin. If I did that I'd be in BIG trouble for sure!

As Aunty Alice puts on her coat, she says to me, "I expect you'll sleep better without these two NOISY lads in your room, won't you, Tom?"

And I say (because it's TRUE), "They're not NOISY. It was both of you SNORING that was NOISY!"

Then I start doing what I think is a very good impression of Uncle Kevin snoring.

SnnnnnOOORRREEE SSSSHHHHHH SSSNNNOOORRREE SSSHHHHHH SSNNOORREE

Luckily for me – Mum and Dad are LAUGHING along with the cousins. Aunty Alice and Uncle Kevin aren't laughing quite as much.

As they leave, we can hear them arguing about who snores the most.

The cousins WAVE goodbye and after they've driven off, Mum says,

"I can't BELIEVE you SNORED like that, Tom!"

(Which makes me think I'm in trouble.)

"It was HILARIOUS!"

OK, I'm not - PHEW.

Mum wants to know if I'd like a

HOT CHOCOLATE.

YES, PLEASE!

As if I'd ever say no.

"You deserve a treat for having the cousins SQUASHED in your room," she tells me.

I agree.

When I get my HOT CHOCOLATE it has marshmallows and chocolate sprinkles too.

YUM!

There's something about the marshmallows that remind me of someone?

Mmmmm, I know.

I push the sprinkles around a bit more with my spoon.

Guess who!

Ha! Ha! Ha!

Now that the cousins have gone, Delia slopes downstairs.

"What's so funny?" she wants to know.

"Nothing," I say, then eat

both my marshmallows.

YUM

Next ... I help myself to **THREE** biscuits.

Only Mum says I have

"too many!"

"They're for

my art

project," I

tell her.

(Which is

quick thinking!)

So I've drawn

around the

1. chocolate

biscuit

2. caramel

wafer

3. custard cream

to make this

monster doodle.

1. Chocolate bisc

2. Caramel wafer

3. Custard cream

(Mum lets me keep the wafer in
the end.)

BACK TO SCHOOL EXTRA & FAST

Since the school closed, Caretaker Stan has been working really hard clearing up the snow.

Hopefully no one will slip over now, he tells us as kids start to arrive.

Though I don't think Mrs Nap heard him.

Whoop!

Slip!

Inside, the school is nice and WARM again (almost too warm). As well as the extra heat, the other thing I notice is ...

MY NEW NEIGHBOUR is sitting at the spare desk.

↓

AMY PORTER is still next to me – so that's a relief. Mr Fullerman says,

"Morning, CLASS 5F."

"Morning, Mr Fullerman,"

we all say back.

"It's a bit warmer than the other day!"

(You can say that again.)

"I'd like you all to give a very BIG Oakfield School WELCOME to June Jones, who's joining our class today — stand up, June."

June stands up and waves at everyone.

I wave a little bit — but not

very enthusiastically.

 asks June where she lives.

Obviously I KNOW the answer to that question but I keep quiet. She and AMY

are chatting; maybe

she won't bother me

too much after all?

Which is EXCELLENT, because I'm going to concentrate on WORK TODAY.

(No, I AM, honestly.)

Solid 😊 thinks there might STILL be a chance for me to get a **STAR PUPIL BADGE.**
He tells me, 😊 "Just try to LOOK like you're working REALLY hard all the time, Tom."
I can do that. *SEE* – here's me pretending to work hard.

work work work

I'm doing fine until Marcus starts saying, 😠 "Tom ... Tom ... **TOM!**"
"What is it, Marcus?" 😠
"You know, I'm a **STAR PUPIL.** I'm going to stay in the library today if it's too cold."
"Good for you, Marcus."
He's about to keep NATTERING
to me, so I tell him,

"I'm trying to concentrate on what
Mr Fullerman is saying. I want to work
really hard. There's a chance I could get a
STAR PUPIL BADGE too."

"What, YOU? I doubt it," Marcus says.
But at least he shuts up and leaves me alone.

Mr Fullerman starts telling us about today's
lesson.

I'm listening.

I'm going to write down a few important
things (as it looks impressive).
Right after I finish doing this doodle.

I've doodled on both my hands.

This one's **M**r **F**ullerman. And this one is Marcus.
Ha! Ha! Ha!

If I move my hand around it looks like he's

 talking.   I can't wait to show Derek
          my hand puppets!

   The other thing I do is fold some of the paper

I've been given to write on into ...

THESE.*

As I'm drawing on the front, **M**r **F**ullerman

says, **"I hope that's not the paper you're**

supposed to be writing on, Tom?"

"No, sir," I say. (It is.)

*See page 222 on how to FOLD a monster from paper.

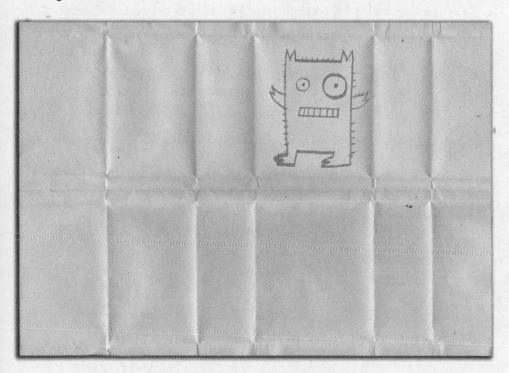

I have to try and unfold the paper monster under the desk and smmmmoooth it out. Which works a tiny bit. Looks like it's going to be <u>ANOTHER</u> wrinkly piece of paper to stick in my book.

I'll turn it over - that might help.

(Mmmmm, not much.

    I can still see my monster. Groan.)

EXTRA SPECIAL LUNCH BREAK

June → hasn't been as annoying as I thought. Which is a RELIEF.

At lunchtime I tell Derek how June sat next to **AMY** in class. (Which is a bit TOO close to me for my liking.)

He says, "Oh no - that's not good."

And I say, "YES, but THESE are GOOD - LOOK!" I show Derek my hand doodles by making them talk.

"Ohh, Mr Fullerman, I SOOO want to be a **STAR PUPIL**. I'm going to be the BEST **STAR PUPIL** EVER!"

"I'm sorry, Marcus, you can't be a **STAR PUPIL** because you are AN IDIOT and we can't have IDIOTS being **STAR PUPILS**!"

"But I want a **BADGE**, Mr FULLERMAN, please can I have a **BADGE**?"

"You can have a **BADGE**, MARCUS - but yours will HAVE to say IDIOT on it and not **STAR**."

I'm making Derek laugh a lot – we both STOP when **M**r **F**ullerman's SHADOW suddenly appears behind us.

"STAR PUPILS don't bring in LATE or wrinkled homework, Tom."

"Yes, **M**r **F**ullerman."

(PHEW, that could have been worse.)

Later on – my doodles come in handy when Marcus starts showing me his **BADGE** (AGAIN). "Take a look, Tom – it's probably the closest you'll get to a **STAR PUPIL BADGE.**"

So I show him my hand doodle and make it say...

"I may have got a

STAR PUPIL BADGE ...

but I'm still an IDIOT."

Which shuts him up.

Back in class, Mr Fullerman is telling us what this lesson's work is. As he's talking, I'm busy making my hand move at the same time. It takes a bit of concentration. I'm not really listening. So when

Mr Fullerman says, **"You know what you have to do now, Class 5F."**

(I don't.)

I glance in Marcus's direction, then in AMY'S. I can see they are writing what looks like a POEM. I try leaning back to see what June is doing and Mr Fullerman says, **"Tom, stop leaning back in your chair and get on with your poem."**

"Yes, sir." I whisper to AMY,

"What's the POEM about?"

 **AMY** says something that sounds like "The **OLD** ". REALLY? I can't ask her again because

Mr Fullerman is looking at me.

Marcus's just written this in his book.

It was one hundred years ago.

So maybe we are writing about The **OLD** ?

I whisper, "Ppppssst, Marcus, are we writing about The **OLD** ?"

And he says, "THE **OLD** ? Errr, yes, Tom, we're writing about The **OLD** ."

So that's what I do.

I don't finish it in class. But I'm allowed to take it home. I've already crossed out a lot of words – so I might have to write it out again on ANOTHER piece of paper and STICK it in my book.

I can do that – no problem.

MY EXTRA BAD WEEK

The GOOD news is I've finished my poem and have written it out VERY neatly on a FRESH piece of paper.

It's all about **THE FOSSILS** (who are very old). I'm hoping I'll get LOADS of MERITS and it might HELP Mr Fullerman decide who to give another **STAR PUPIL BADGE** to. (☺ ← ME.)

The **BAD** news is ... the rest of my week doesn't go quite so well.

FIRSTLY, the **SNOW** has started to **MELT** (turns out the "storms" weren't that bad after all. Which is a shame). It's mostly been fun.

Then Amy was asked by Mr Fullerman to help June make friends. So she kept on trying to get June to ˎtalkˎ to ME.

I made a **BIG effort** by asking June what bands she liked.

When I told her I liked **DUDE 3** , she pulled a funny face like there was something WRONG with them!

AND (if that wasn't bad enough) when I got home Mum had made a DELICIOUS CAKE. I was just about to TRY a piece when she **shouted**,

DON'T TOUCH IT!

"It's not for you, it's for the new NEIGHBOURS!" I had to WATCH Mum TAKE the cake round to June's house – which was VERY HARD to do.

NO

And (it gets WORSE) when Mum came back she was **FURIOUS** ...

WITH ME!

"What have I done NOW?" I said. Mum took out the NEW HOME CARD she'd given to them and said ...

"This was supposed to be a NICE welcome to your NEW HOME card, with a little sorry message from you."

 "That's what I did," I told Mum.

Then she showed me the card.
"Which bit of <u>this</u> is an apology, then?"

I'm NOT
Sorry for the

loud music.
I'm going to do it again.
From Tom

Ha! Ha!

Congratulations on
your New Home.

Love from the Gates
family (next door),
Rita, Frank,
Tom and Delia x

From the Gates cousins

It took me a while to convince her I didn't WRITE it. "The cousins did it when they signed the card - not me."

Mum made me sign ANOTHER card.

I asked her if she could make ANOTHER cake too? For us!

Nice try, Tom.

(It was worth asking. Groan.)

After that, I went to my room and GUESS who I saw sitting in the garden eating a MASSIVE piece of cake ?

Yes, that's right. JUNE.

Why would you eat cake in the garden unless you just wanted me to see it?

I tried really hard not to care...

Who wants cake anyway? cake (Me.)

we're doing the FAMILY PORTRAIT for **THE FOSSILS'** **fiftieth*** *wedding anniversary*.

Groan.

Uncle Kevin has sent over instructions on EVERYTHING:

 • How to get there

• WHAT to wear

• To remember to SMILE! ☺

"Good luck with that," Dad says as he looks at Delia.

Mum suggests we could pretend the list didn't arrive in time?

"Good idea," Dad agrees.

(Scrunched-up list) Delia isn't happy about the photo at all. She warns us in advance.

"Just so you know, the sunglasses are staying **ON**."

(I've seen Delia without her sunglasses* – she looks scary.) *See page 6, Genius Ideas (Mostly).

When we get to the FAMILY PORTRAIT studio,
Uncle Kevin, Aunty Alice and the cousins are
EARLY and waiting for us.

"They're wearing matching clothes,"
I whisper to Mum.

"Colour coordinated too,"
Dad adds.

The first thing
Uncle Kevin says is,
"Didn't you get my NOTES?"

Dad says, "No - are you sure you sent them?"
Which makes Uncle Kevin wonder if he did.

Then he gets distracted by the photographer.

Who seems to be very **excited** about today.
He says,

> **Let's make this a FUN and memorable day, shall we?**

Which makes Delia even more grumpy.
(If that's possible.)

> You've got to be KIDDING?

she moans.

Uncle **K**evin asks the photographer the
first (of many) questions about what camera
Really? he's using.

"I'm a keen photographer,"
he tells him.

Delia keeps texting her friends and muttering
comments like: "This is TRAGIC."

— "What am I even doing here?"

The photographer is having quite a hard time
already arranging everyone together.

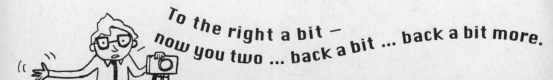

To the right a bit —
now you two ... back a bit ... back a bit more.

Uncle Kevin complains that if we'd all got his notes, this would have been easier.

— Tom - no bunny ears
— Groan
Not working

The cousins end up at the back because they are so HUGE. Delia won't smile AT ALL and Dad wants to keep his hat on but Uncle Kevin keeps taking it off.

"Don't touch MY HAT!"

Dad tells him in a cross voice.

The photographer keeps taking pictures.

"Can everyone at least TRY and look a little bit happy?"

He's doing his best.

Finally he tells us, **"That's it - I've got enough photos!"** (He sounds relieved.)

We're about to leave when Aunty Alice shouts,
"NOT YET!" then gets out a selection
of Granny Mavis's "KNIT WEAR".
"She'd LOVE a photo of all the
grandchildren together wearing something
she's lovingly made for you."

Delia thinks it's a **stupid** idea.

"SERIOUSLY, we look ridiculous enough."

Mum gives her a scarf and says,
"Just do it or we'll be here even longer."

So we put on the hats and scarves, and
even though the cousins are messing around,
we do the picture.

"Granny Mavis and
Granddad Bob will be THRILLED," Aunty Alice tells us.

I'm just PLEASED it's all OVER.

(I'm not the only one.)

This was WORSE than having a

school photo* done.

Dad's been sent all the

photos from the FAMILY PORTRAIT photo session.

Which was ~~£1~~ QUICK.

They have to choose which one to give

as a present. Mum's in the shed

with Dad looking at them on the computer.

I go in to have a

look as well.

*See page 78, The Brilliant
World of Tom Gates.

"I look AWFUL in that one!" Mum gasps.

"Yes, but look at Uncle Kevin's expression there!" Dad says.

Delia looks the same in ALL the pictures. Dad says, "How about we have some fun and make a few changes to everyone on the computer ... apart from me, of course." YEAH.

It takes him a while – but the end result is

"Very funny," Mum says, but she's not keen on the moustache he's given her.

The cousins look like vampires.

"Make Uncle Kevin's teeth BIGGER," I suggest.

He looks like a rabbit!

(I can see where I get my doodling skills from now.)

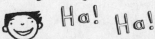
Ha! Ha!

Ha!
Ha!

Ha!
Ha!

Eventually after we've stopped laughing, Mum and Dad CHOOSE a **nice** picture of ALL of us, to send off for printing and to be put in a fancy frame for **THE FOSSILS'** present.

It's NOT my idea of an EXTRA special present, but I'm sure **THE FOSSILS** will like it.

Lovely

I hope they like the doodle card I'm going to do as well. I could write my poem inside it too? (Because I am a nice grandson.) ☺

EXTRA HOMEWORK

I'm forced to wear Granny's mittens again, as it's still a bit chilly. I keep my hands in my pockets most of the time so people can't see or LAUGH at them.

Ha! Ha!

I'm with Derek in the school playground waiting to go inside when Norman comes over. We're all chatting about the band and how DOGZOMBIES need to do MORE practising and play some GIGS.

"We've been saying that for ages," Derek says. (Which is true.)

"But THIS time we really have to do it," I tell them. Derek reminds us that the school OPEN DAY is coming up. "If Mr Keen asks us to play at the OPEN DAY for the new parents – we should say YES."

174

Mr Keen has asked **DOGZOMBIES** to play at the school concert before. It's a good idea. Norman agrees. "DEFINITELY say YES!"

"OK, I will – but I might not JUMP around like that, Norman," I tell him.

Back in class, Mr Fullerman reminds us about the OPEN DAY and OUR POEMS.

"I hope everyone brought them in?"

he says.

NO! NO! NO!

What did I do with my POEM? I know it's somewhere around. I look in my exercise book to see if I was sensible and stuck it in as soon as I'd finished it.

AND GUESS WHAT? I didn't.

I'm sure it's on a piece of paper somewhere? Mr Fullerman says,

"I'd like some of you to read out your poems to the class."

AMY has already got her book out and open.

Her poem is called

"FROZEN SNOW".

She sees me looking at her book, so I say, "I HAVE done mine, I just can't find it."

I start looking in my bag and rustle around a bit more.

EVENTUALLY I find it in my history book.

Whooop! Whooop! I have my homework. PHEW!

YES, it's written on a very wrinkled-up piece of paper, but at least I HAVE it.

Mr Fullerman sees me WAFTING it around and asks,

"Is that another scrunched-up bit of homework, Tom?"

So I say, "Yes, Mr Fullerman, but I did work really hard, and it wasn't easy writing a WHOLE poem about THE OLD."

Mr Fullerman looks a bit puzzled.

Marcus is chuckling to himself, so I ask him, "What's so funny?"

He says, "Nothing." Which makes me suspicious. His poem is called "MY **SUPER SLEDGE**".

I ask him, "What's <u>that</u> got to do with 'The OLD'?" Which makes Marcus laugh a bit more.

Then he says, "NOTHING, because you were supposed to write a poem about THE COLD, not THE OLD. Bad luck, Tom."

I'm trying to think 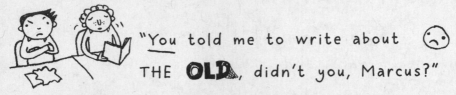 back to
WHY I have got muddled up.

OK ... just remembered.

"You told me to write about
THE OLD, didn't you, Marcus?"

I remind him.

Marcus shrugs his shoulders at me.

"I don't remember."

He's SO annoying. I suppose I could swap

a few words around when I read it?

As I'm wondering what to do,

Mr Fullerman says,

**"TOM, would you like to read
your poem out to the class?"**

(Not really.)

Ha! Ha! Ha!

I take a deep breath and say,

"Mr Fullerman, it's like THIS. I made a mistake and wrote my poem about being **OLD**, not COLD."

Everyone starts laughing (especially Marcus). Then I have a BRAINWAVE and I hold up my WRINKLED paper and explain,

"I DELIBERATELY SCRUNCHED up the paper to make it LOOK WRINKLED like a REAL **OLD** 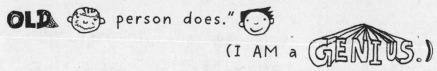 person does."

(I AM a GENIUS.)

Then I read out my poem and Mr Fullerman really likes it!

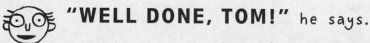 **"WELL DONE, TOM!"** he says.

(Thank you, thank you.)

I'll stick my poem in my book later.
Here's some SPACE for Mr Fullerman to
write something nice and give me LOTS
of MERITS.

(Fingers crossed.)

WELL done, Tom.

You've earned 5 MERITS for
your "OLD" poem.
Mr Fullerman

RESULT! ☆

When Marcus read out his poem, he
thought it was BRILLIANT.

(It wasn't.)

Mr Fullerman only gave him ONE MERIT. So
I told him that ONE MERIT was better than
NONE. Then I left out my book so he could
see I had FIVE MERITS for mine.

Tee hee.

I am enjoying retelling my POEM story to Derek and Norman as we put on our coats for home time.

Every time I put on Granny's mittens I think, "I must get some new gloves."

Mr Keen is standing by the door saying **goodbye** to everyone when Derek reminds me that we were going to SAY YES if he asked for **DOGZOMBIES** to play at the OPEN DAY, even though it's tomorrow.

We smile at Mr Keen and he says, **Bye, everyone.** And that's it. Nothing else.

"Let's go back and ask him," Norman says.

Good idea. All three of us walk back to Mr Keen.

He says, **"Forgotten something, boys?"**

Norman says, "Mr Keen, Tom's got something to ask you."

(Thanks, Norman.)

"Well, sir ... can our band - **DOGZOMBIES** - play at the school OPEN DAY tomorrow?"

Mr Keen says, **"That's a GREAT idea!"** Which gets our hopes up. Then he tells us, **"But I've already got Mr Sprocket's orchestra playing. You can play next year, I promise."**

Oh well, we tried.

"We'd be SO much better than Mr Sprocket's orchestra," Derek says as we walk home. "They'll put kids off coming to our school," I tell them.

"**DOGZOMBIES ROCK**," Norman says before heading off home in the other direction. Derek and I agree to concentrate on learning a few more songs too.

"**DOGZOMBIES** would rock more if we practised," I tell Derek before going inside my house.

I'm sure the NEW copy of ROCK WEEKLY is out today? I take a look in Delia's room just in case she's bought it.

YES, it's THERE. I borrow it to read in my room before she gets home. When I SPOT this competition inside the magazine - I take it as a SIGN. It's like it was MEANT to be for us.

BAND BATTLE!

Are you in a BAND?
Then this competition is for YOU.

We'll be holding auditions around the country.
Come along and PLAY LIVE with your band.
If you get voted through to the next round,
the prize is to PERFORM at the

ROCK WEEKLY FESTIVAL

along with some of our FAVOURITE rock bands.

See below for more details.

DOGZOMBIES, HERE WE COME!

EXTRA GOOD School OPEN DAY

Mr Fullerman asked me to come and help on the OPEN DAY and I said YES 😊 straight away because:

1. It might help me get a **STAR PUPIL** badge.

2. He said there would be free orange juice, CAKE and BISCUITS!

Oakfield School **OPEN DAY** is for grown-ups and kids who might want to come to this school in the future. **OUR** job is SIMPLE. We've been told to BE on OUR BEST BEHAVIOUR and **TRY HARD** [not] to put off anyone from coming here.

This school is great (Some kids try harder than others.)

Don't look

CLASS 5W

I'm here with all the **STAR PUPILS:**

Amy, Leroy and Indrani, Florence and Mark Clump
(that means Marcus is here too).

We're showing people around the
school and telling them how GOOD it is
to be here.

Look at my badge

Which is HARD work.

(I don't tell anyone that I came to OAKFIELD School
because Delia went here and it wasn't far to walk.)

I've brought the BAND BATTLE
competition page with me to show Derek and
Norman, forgetting they're not here.

So I show it to AMY instead.

"We're going to ENTER this competition,"
I tell her. "Do you think DOGZOMBIES could win it?"

"I've seen the posters in town, it's a
BIG competition – so you probably won't
win," she says.   (Oh, OK.)

185

"**DOGZOMBIES** need a challenge," I explain.

"Really?" **AMY** says, like she's not convinced.

"**M**r Keen really wanted us to play for the OPEN DAY today. We said no thanks, but maybe we'll do it next year," I tell her just as Mr Sprocket's recycled orchestra begins to play in the hall.

"We'd be **much** better than them," I add.

"I hope so," **AMY** says before she helps some parents find the library.

Our classroom looks a lot better than normal. **M**r **F**ullerman has made a **BIG effort** to have interesting things displayed on the walls for OPEN DAY. Like my POEM. (That doesn't happen very often.) ☺

I'm hovering around near it in case anyone wants to ask me any questions about it.

I'm also doing IMPRESSIVE smiling at new parents and kids at the same time.

POEMS By Class 5F

186

My smiling seems to be working — because
Mr Fullerman notices me and tells some parents,
"This is TOM, who's written this excellent poem on the wall. Would you show this family where Mrs Worthington's classroom is, please?"
"YES, SIR," I say
(thinking about my possible STAR PUPIL BADGE).

On the way to the classroom, the parents ask me a few questions, like:
"Do you like this school then, Tom?"
So I say,
"YES, especially now the **HEATING'S** working again. Mind you, we did get a day off school when it broke down, so THAT was good."

(All true.)

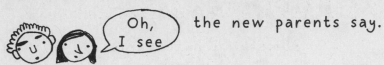 Oh, I see the new parents say.

Next they want to know who's playing the ♪ MUSIC in the hall?

"It's sort of **MUSIC**. That's Mr Sprocket's school orchestra and everything they play is ACTUALLY ALL RuBBISH."

"I don't think they sound *THAT* bad?" the dad tells me.

I'm about to explain it's the INSTRUMENTS that are MADE of RUBBISH when we get to Mrs Worthington's class.

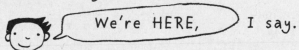 We're HERE, I say.

The boy wants to know if Mrs Worthington is ☺ a NICE teacher?

I'm **VERY** helpful and tell him something important.

"She's a great teacher and quite nice as **long** as you DON'T mention her **MOUSTACHE**."

(I probably shouldn't have said that – but it's too late now.)

I'm on my way back to the classroom when I get distracted by the **FREE** cake and biscuits that are in the hall. I think I deserve a snack. It won't take long to help myself to a biscuit or two.

Mmmmmm. What shall I have? I'm trying to decide when Marcus nips in and takes the custard cream I had my eye on.

MINE, he says.

"Because I have a **STAR PUPIL BADGE**," he adds.

(Yawn, yawn...)

Mr Sprocket comes over to ask us BOTH a question.

"Can one of you TWO **STAR PUPILS** close that door over there, please? It's letting the rain in." MR SPROCKET THINKS I'M A **STAR PUPIL!**

"Yes, Mr Sprocket, I <u>WILL</u>," I say, and set off for the door.

"He means ME, Tom, I'm the only **STAR PUPIL** here," Marcus says.

"No need, I'm going, Marcus," I tell him, and then we both end up doing F A S T *walking* to the door.

I get there first and try to close the door.

PUSH

Marcus manages to SHOVE me outside and pulls the door closed behind me. It's POURING with rain and I'm getting WET. I'm pushing the door and telling him to LET me in!

Marcus makes a face at me, holding the door shut. "Ha! Ha! Are you getting wet, Tom?" he laughs.

YES I am, BUT...

I can see who's standing behind Marcus.

A LOUD, BOOMY voice says,

"LET GO OF THE DOOR, MARCUS."

He stops laughing.

It's Mr Fullerman and he's
NOT PLEASED.

I come in from outside looking a bit ... damp.

Mr Fullerman tells Marcus,

"Star pupils should NOT be misbehaving, especially on OPEN DAY, Marcus."

"Yes, Mr Fullerman," he says.

"Now apologize to Tom."

I'm waiting, Marcus.

Still waiting (and dripping).

"I'm sorry for pushing you out of the door, Tom."

He doesn't look that sorry.

I start COUGHING a bit loudly, so he has to say it again. It was worth getting rained on just to hear Marcus say sorry to me, twice. ☺

(This OPEN DAY has been a success.)

The next day in school we have MATHS first and then a spelling test after (which I forgot about). AMY swaps her answers with June to get them marked. I swap mine with Marcus, who's still annoyed he had to say sorry to me. We're marking each other's spellings when I spot Marcus has spelt the word POURING wrong. ✗ "It's spelt like ... 'It's POURING with rain, I'm sorry I pushed you in it, Tom' – remember?"

Marcus is trying hard not to. — Hmmmphhh.

AMY and June have swapped their spellings back and are chatting. I start listening in when I HEAR Amy say the word **music.**

She says, "Tom knows lots about music."

(Do I?)

Then as I've given Marcus back his spellings (he got three wrong), and I've got mine back (two wrong), I try and make a BIG effort with June and join in the conversation. Which doesn't go well.

This is what happened.

Me: "What kind of music do you like, June?"

June: "Good music."

Me: "Me too... I like **DUDE 3**, who are the **BEST BAND** in the **WHOLE** WORLD."

June: "NO WAY - **DUDE3** ARE RUBBISH."

Me: ....← (lost for words)

Me: "They're **BRILLIANT**, are you **NUTS**? Have you **H**eard them?"

June: "Yes. That's why I think they're rubbish."

AMY: "Calm down, you two."

 Me: "My band **DOGZOMBIES** are like them because they're **SO** good."

June: "Your band must be 'rubbish' as well if you're like **DUDE3** ."

I'm saved by the SCHOOL BELL.

June pulls a silly face 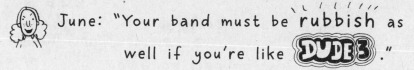 and leaves ...

I'm SHOCKED.

At break time Derek and Norman ask me about the **BAND BATTLE!** ←competition.

I still have the page torn out of Delia's **ROCK WEEKLY** in my pocket. It's a bit **WRINKLED** but I show it to them.

 "We should enter," Norman says.

"With a bit more practice, we can do the **live** audition, can't we?" I wonder.

"Let's play 'Delia's a Weirdo'; we know that song really well," Derek suggests.

"We could **WIN**," Norman shouts, getting carried away.

I don't think we could **WIN**, BUT when Marcus comes over I change my mind.

"WIN WHAT?"

"This BAND BATTLE!

competition. DOGZOMBIES are going to

enter it," I tell him.

Marcus looks at the competition and says,

"You've got NO chance; all the best

bands enter that."

"We're a good band!" I say.

"That new girl June said you were a

RUBBISH band, I heard her."

What? (That's not exactly what June said.)

Suddenly NORMAN SHOUTS,

DOGZOMBIES ROCK

and I say, "EXACTLY, we do, and we're

going to TRY and win."

(I hope.)

Marcus points to his **STAR PUPIL BADGE** and tells us, "Yeah, yeah – whatever. And by the way, you can't stand there, you're blocking the doorway."

He's SSSSSHHHHing us to [move.]

Groan.

Marcus goes on, "As a **STAR PUPIL**, it's my job to help keep the doorways clear."

"Really?"

(I'm sure it's NOT part of his job.)

We all take one step to the [right] just to shut him up.

We're not standing in the doorway any more.

Marcus shows us his badge **AGAIN.**

(As if we haven't seen

it **enough.**)

Back at home I STILL can't believe that 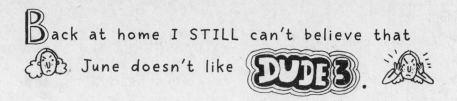 June doesn't like **DUDE 3**.

Now I know that, every time I go into my bedroom I put on THEIR ALBUM.

Not really **loud**, just loud enough that she might be able to hear it through the wall. I'm hoping that EVENTUALLY she'll get to like them. (That's my plan.)

The only problem with playing **DUDE 3** a little bit loud is that I'm supposed to be doing my homework and it's tricky to concentrate when I **HAVE** to keep stopping to do some SERIOUS AIR guitar moves. I have to turn it down a bit.

I need to get this done, as it might help me get my own **STAR PUPIL BADGE**. I've got a GOOD chance now after what happened to Marcus.

He let the POWER of the badge go to his head a bit and got caught making fun of us from the window of the library.

He was inside (and warm).

We were outside (and cold).

Miss Page, the librarian, wasn't impressed, and Mr Fullerman wasn't happy either.

Not again, Marcus!

I wonder how many times he can get into trouble before Mr Fullerman will take away his badge?

If he does lose it – I can think of a few badges he could wear. Like these...

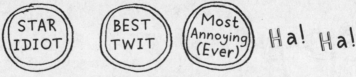

(STAR IDIOT)   (BEST TWIT)   (Most Annoying (Ever))   Ha! Ha!

Better finish my homework AND the card for **THE FOSSILS** as well.

200

EXTRA SPECIAL CELEBRATIONS

* *

With everything that's been going on at school, Granny Mavis and Granddad Bob's *fiftieth wedding anniversary* has ⇒ ⇒ ⇒ **ZOOMED** around really fast. They *think* they're going to have **tea** and **biscuits** with a few of their friends at the

LEAFY GREEN OLD FOLKS' HOME.

⟨WRONG!⟩

It's a **BIG** **SURPRISE** ★ **PARTY** with everybody coming.

201

I nearly told Granddad about the *PARTY* the other day when I said ...

"I'll see you on Saturday, Granddad!"

"Saturday, what's happening Saturday?"

"NOTHING, Granddad."

"Are you sure?"

"YES, it's just a plain old Saturday. Nothing is happening at ALL."

It was a close call. (Phew.)

Keeping this party a secret has <u>NOT</u> been easy.

We're going over to the LEAFY GREEN OLD FOLKS' HOME EARLY so we can be there when THE FOSSILS arrive.

I'm quite EXCITED about the *PARTY* now.

Delia wants to go out with her friends and is **NOT** very excited at all.

Mum says, "It's your grandparents' anniversary - you can't **miss** it."

Dad makes a suggestion. "Invite your friends to the **PARTY** if you want. I'm sure Granny and Granddad won't mind."

Delia says, "I MIND! I'm [not] asking my FRIENDS to a party at an OLD folks' home!" OLD folk

Dad says, "They throw a good party, it'll be FUN!"

Delia stomps off to the car clutching Mum's phone, still grumbling.

Delia →

When we get to the LEAFY GREEN OLD FOLKS' HOME, we can tell everyone's been VERY busy.

There's loads of delicious food and CAKES laid
out already and the hall's decorated too.

(This is where **DOGZOMBIES** played their first ever GIG*, but it didn't look like this when we played here.)

Dad has already collected the FAMILY PORTRAIT, which is now |framed| and wrapped up with a BIG bow on it.

Mum says, "Did it l👁👁k OK?"

"A STUNNING work of ART,"

Dad tells her. Which would be a surprise, as <u>none</u> of the photos were that good before.

THE FOSSILS have been asked by their best friend, Buster, to come for a small tea.

He's told them that most of the home will be out playing (bingo.)

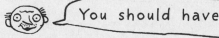

You should have SEEN their faces!

he adds, laughing.

*See page 296, Excellent Excuses (And Other Good Stuff), for the full story.

Uncle Kevin and the rest
of the family are all here.
(Early as usual.)
"You're looking very smart," Dad says to him.
"You're looking like you," Uncle Kevin says back.
Which is just the way Dad likes it.
Looks like the **WHOLE** of LEAFY
GREEN have come to the party, along with
some of **THE FOSSILS**' other friends too.
Mum's just got a message from Buster saying
they're on their way. So everyone shuffles
into the corner of the hall to hide.

Dad suggests that it might be TOO much
of a SHOCK if we all LEAP OUT and
SHOUT

SURPRISE at them!
I hadn't thought about that.
"EVERYONE should WAVE and SMILE a LOT."
So that's what we do when **THE FOSSILS** arrive...

We just couldn't help ourselves.

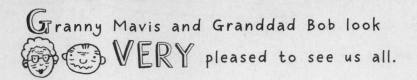Granny Mavis and Granddad Bob look VERY pleased to see us all.

"Isn't this lovely!"

she says, hugging me.

"Time to get STUCK into the food,"

the cousins say.

Delia is already asking if she can leave to

meet her friends. "Not until after they've had their presents,"

Mum tells her.

Uncle Kevin wants to make a (speech,)

but he's FORCED to cut it short, as

Vera, who's sitting near him, keeps

nodding off and snoring.

zzzz
zzzzz
zzzzzzzzzz

Which is FUNNY.

"I won't take it personally!"

Uncle Kevin laughs awkwardly.

(Taking it personally.) Ha! Ha!

Then he gives **THE FOSSILS** the picture.

"Here's a little family present from us. And the **BIG** present over there is from EVERYONE."

He's pointing at the LARGE present hidden under a brightly coloured tablecloth.

Granddad Bob is looking at the wrapped-up box and says, "Is that a new set of teeth for me?"

I nudge Mum and say, "I told you he needed new teeth!"

They undo the bow and open the box and inside is the VERY special FAMILY PORTRAIT ...

... the WRONG family portrait.

Luckily **THE FOSSILS** see the funny  side of it.

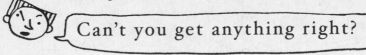 **U**nlike Aunty Alice and Uncle Kevin. They're NOT happy with Dad at all.

 Can't you get anything right?

(They're not happy with the bunny ears, vampire teeth or moustaches he's given them either.)

Dad says, "There's obviously been a mix-up."

"Really, how can you tell?" Delia says while taking some photos. Mum's shaking her head. Me and the cousins think it's the FUNNIEST thing we've ever seen.

And so do all of

LEAFY GREEN OLD FOLKS' HOME.

(Apart from Vera – who's still asleep.) zzzzzz

Mum suggests they should open their OTHER present from all of us.

Which is a BIG HIT.

WOW

I get some cake first (before the cousins EAT everything), then give THE FOSSILS the card I've drawn.

"There's a poem inside too. I wrote it. Sorry about the crinkled paper," I tell them.

I hope they like it.

My Grandparents are

OLD

By Tom Gates (who is quite young).

Here are **THE FOSSILS**,

you can see.

They are quite **OLD**

and rickety.

With Granddad Bob

you must be patient.

Because he says,

 I'm getting ancient.

My Granny Mavis

feels FINE! Yippee!

For someone

who is NINETY-NINE.

(I think she's only eighty-three,

she keeps her age a MYSTERY.)

THE FOSSILS are
quite small and **WRINKLED**
With 👵 hair that's grey
and skin that's *crinkled*.

No need to use
a walking 🦯 STICK.

Their mobile scooter
Does the **TRICK**.

They do their shopping on it weekly
as Granddad's knees are slightly creaky.

And now we're CELEBRATING

with some TEA.

Their FIFTIETH ANNIVERSARY!

But as they're OLD,

it won't end late.

They'll be asleep zzzzzz

by half past eight.

THE END ➡️

Love from your
favourite grandson,
Tom xx

They really do like it a LOT.

The bit in my poem about **THE FOSSILS**
being asleep at eight-thirty doesn't happen.
The party goes on for a while.

(Even Delia ends up staying longer than
she thought she would.)

EXTRA
SPECIAL
TREATS

not

No more **FREEZING** outside for me!

I have GOOD NEWS.

It's only for the last few weeks of term

but **M**r **F**ullerman has made me a

STAR PUPIL too.  YEAH!

(Marcus still has his badge, but only JUST.

Mr **F**ullerman told him **"No more**

nonsense" or he'll take it away.)

I was VERY pleased to read this, though. ⟶

Well done, Tom, for
some EXCELLENT (if a bit wrinkled)
homework this term.
And a FANTASTIC poem.
Come and see me at the end
of the week
to pick up your STAR PUPIL BADGE.

Mr Fullerman

And ... drum roll ...

here it is.

Granny Mavis brought round this TIN
of SWEETS as a thank-you for
the party and presents.

I got VERY EXCITED ...

Superior SWEETS

Mmmmm mmmmm mmmmmm

... until I opened the tin.

And saw this.

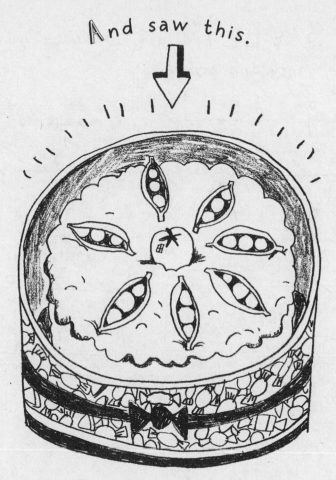

It's Granny's home-made VEGETABLE CAKE!

Oh well...

(Extra SPECIAL TREATS ... not.)

Make a stand-up MONSTER

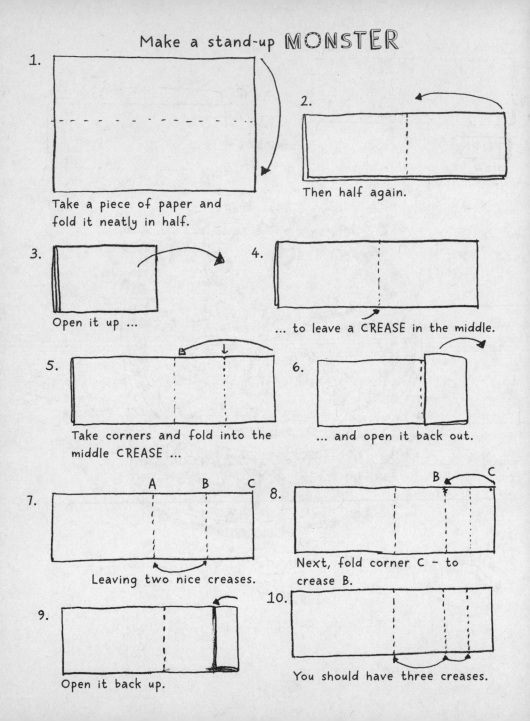

1. Take a piece of paper and fold it neatly in half.

2. Then half again.

3. Open it up ...

4. ... to leave a CREASE in the middle.

5. Take corners and fold into the middle CREASE ...

6. ... and open it back out.

7. A B C
   Leaving two nice creases.

8. Next, fold corner C – to crease B.

9. Open it back up.

10. You should have three creases.

11.

TURN over the paper and draw your monster in this section – don't draw right up to the edge, though.

12.

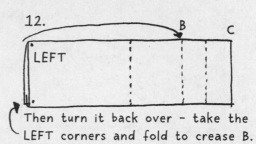

LEFT

B   C

Then turn it back over – take the LEFT corners and fold to crease B.

13.

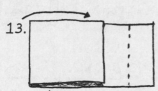

Make a nice crease again, then open it back up.

14.

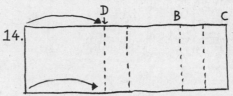

D   B   C

Then one more fold to the new crease D you've just made.

15.

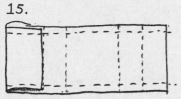

Press down – but this time DON'T unfold it.

16.

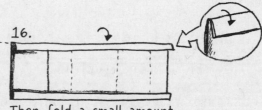

Then fold a small amount of paper over at the top and bottom.

17.

and slot one edge over the other to keep rigid.

FOLD the monster to look like the picture

18.

Ta dah

It should look like this!

LOOK!

Make your monsters into a GAME.

Add numbers to them and use a  scrunched-up

piece of paper as a ball to knock them over

with (like skittles).

The WINNER is the one with the most

POINTS!

RESULT!

Here are some more paper skittles with
different pictures drawn on them...

Ha! Ha!

Tom Gates' Glossary

(Which means explanations for stuff
that might sound a bit ODD.)

Yum!  Biscuits = cookies.

Caramel wafers: 'Excellent' biscuits (cookies)
covered in chocolate with layers of caramel
and wafer inside.

CROSS = ((:U)) angry.

Dodgy = something that's a bit ODD or wrong.
Maybe slightly peculiar or not quite right. For
instance: That apple looks a bit **Dodgy**.
That monster looks
a bit dodgy.

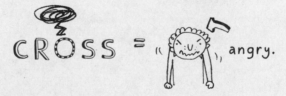

(worm)

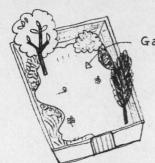 Garden is a YARD

 Jumper / Sweater

A LORRY is a truck

MERITS are special POINTS or STARS awarded by your teacher for excellent work.

Rumbled! basically means **You're busted!**

Rubbish

Garbage

Sledging is the same as sledding

Spanners are wrenches

Sweets = Candy

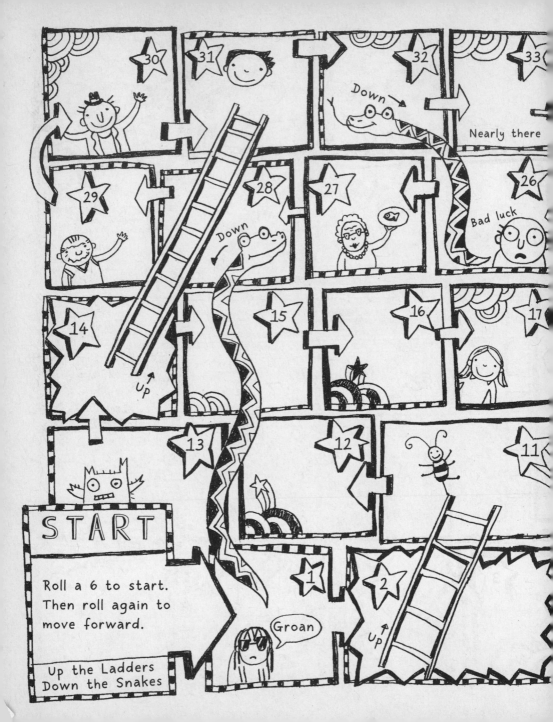

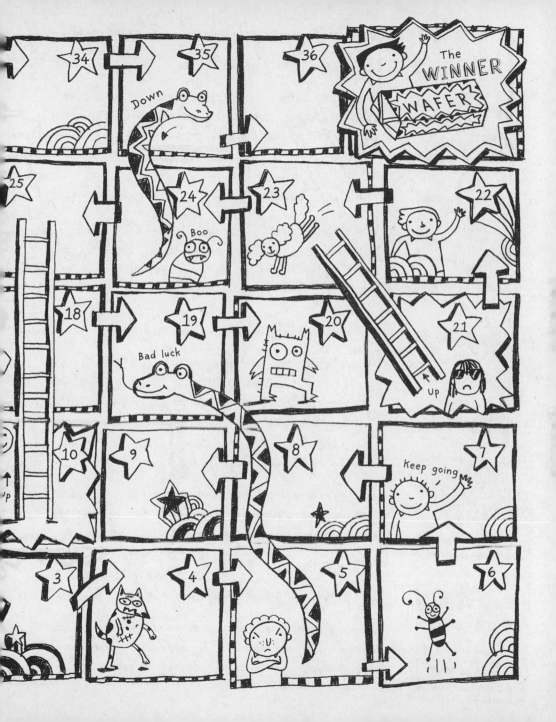

Read More Tom Gates

ISBN 978-1-4431-1936-8

The Brilliant World of Tom Gates

Meet Tom Gates — a master of excuses, an expert doodler, a comic story writer extraordinaire, and the bane of his teacher's existence!

ISBN 978-1-4431-2439-3

Tom Gates: Excellent Excuses (and other good stuff)

Tom Gates is back — and making the most of his holiday! No school for two whole weeks leaves Tom with tons of time for the important things in life. Of course, he still has to do his book report for Mr. Keen . . .

ISBN 978-1-4431-2491-1

Tom Gates: Everything's Amazing (sort of)

Things are better than ever! Well, sort of . . . Back to school, but it's not all bad. Sports Day, the school fair, and Tom's birthday are all coming up. And even better, his big sister Delia won't be at any of those events!

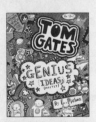

ISBN 978-1-4431-3303-6

Tom Gates: Genius Ideas (mostly)

Seeing Delia without her sunglasses on is a big shock for Tom, but that's nothing compared to the surprise that Dad has in store with his new-found fitness regime!

ISBN 978-1-4431-3366-1

Tom Gates Is Absolutely Fantastic (at some things)

Exciting news! Tom's class is going on the School Activity Trip! That should be fun as long as Tom doesn't get stuck in a group with anyone who snores or, worse still, with . . . Marcus Meldrew.